D0045008

GOLDEN BOYS

GOLDEN BOYS

SONYA HARTNETT

CANDLEWICK PRESS

This is a work of fiction. Names, characters, places, and incidents are either products of the author's imagination or, if real, are used fictitiously.

First U.S. edition 2016

First published by Penguin Group (Australia) 2014

Library of Congress Catalog Card Number 2015937231
ISBN 978-0-7636-7949-1

16 17 18 19 20 21 BVG 10 9 8 7 6 5 4 3 2 1

Printed in Berryville, VA, U.S.A.

This book was typeset in Garamond.

Candlewick Press
99 Dover Street
Somerville, Massachusetts 02144

visit us at www.candlewick.com

For my own sisters and brothers

With their father, there's always a catch: the truth is enough to make Colt take a step back. There's always some small cruelty, an unpleasant little hoop to be crawled through before what's good may begin: here is a gift, but first you must guess its colour. Colt's instinct is to warn his brother—*Bastian, don't*—as if away from a cliff's edge or some quaggy sinkhole, but doing so risks leaving him stranded, alone like someone fallen overboard in the night, watching a boat full of revellers sail on. Bastian will want to play. Their mother will say, in her voice of reined-in dismay, "It's just a bit of fun."

As the eldest he gets to guess first, so he guesses, "Blue."

Their father shakes his head happily. "Nope! Bas?"

Bastian is prone to birdiness, his whole world one of those plastic kitchens in which girls make tea from petals and water. He guesses, "Yellow?" as though it's perfectly possible their father would bring home for his two boys a bicycle coloured yellow.

"Nope again!" Their father is cheered, rather than nonplussed, by the attempt. "Colt?"

Already Colt feels they've run out of colours. "Green?"

"Not green. Your guess, Bas."

Colt lets his shoulders fall. He looks at his mother, who is lingering by the leather recliner where their father would be sitting if he wasn't standing by the mantelpiece conducting this game. She wears an apron, like a mother on a television show, and doesn't look at him, although she surely feels it, his stare that is leaden even to him. And it happens again, like the clear tinging of a bell, the eerie moment when a truth breaks from the green depths into sunlight: she'll ignore Colt for the rest of his life, if the choice is between her husband and her son. His mother will cling tight to the rail of the boat. Bastian's saying, "Spotty?" and Colt, dazed, stares down at his own feet. He wonders if this is what growing up is—this unbuckling of faith, the isolation. He is only twelve, but he's not afraid. He is old enough. He looks at his brother, laughs rustily. "Spotty? Bas."

Bastian lifts his face. "Why not?"

"Have you ever seen a spotty bike?"

"I mean, all different colours—"

Colt shakes his head; his brother can be unbelievable. "It's not spotty."

"Who knows?" cries their father, reeling them back. "Who knows what's possible? But it isn't spotty. Your guess, Colt."

Colt rummages for colours—he can't remember any they've already nominated, feels only an indignation which, if it had a colour, would be a swampy scarlet. "I don't know. I give up."

"If you give up, you mightn't get the bike . . ."

"Don't give up, Colly!" Bastian bounces on his toes.

Colt draws a breath. He wants to shout at his father that he doesn't care, that no bicycle is worth this humiliation, that he's not some prideless puppet. His mother has turned to him, her gaze reaching across the water, willing him to guess again: he swallows, as if it were icy air and salt water, her refusal to share or even acknowledge his affront. *It doesn't matter,* he wants to yell. *I can be alone.* He's not yet that courageous, but he will be. "Black?"

"Not black. Bastian?"

"Oh, I know, Dad! Purple?"

"Purple it is not. Colt?"

"Red," Colt snaps.

"Not red. It's difficult! Your turn, Bas."

"Is it brown?" asks the boy.

"Sorry, Bas, not brown. Colt?"

This can't go on all night, but it threatens to. The time has come to draw a knife through it. Colt digs his toes into the carpet and thinks about all the bicycles he's seen. At his old school—already it seems a place from a lifetime ago, although if he returned now his friends would hardly have missed him, familiar books would be open, the same papers would be pinned to noticeboards in the corridors, it would be as if he'd never left—the boys had hooked their bikes to the chain-mesh fence, posing them like skeletal carousel horses with their front wheels bucked off the ground. Expensive bikes, all of them, and when they were not the most costly they were still the most fashionable, racers with curved handlebars and tyres as thin as plate. Colt and Bastian have, in fact, such a bicycle each already, neat speedsters which at this moment are safe in the shed and in perfect working order, as their father maintains them. Two boys, two bikes, no need for this mysterious third; but their father heaps gifts upon them, there is nothing the brothers don't receive. Everything they own must be the biggest, the better, the one which glitters most. Suddenly convinced of it, Colt says, "Silver."

And although he's sure his father must shout *yes! silver!* what he actually says, with no sign of wearying, is, "Not silver. Bassy?" Frustration rears crazily, before Colt can crush it. "Dad! Just tell us! Bastian can't guess anymore!"

"Of course he can—"

"I can!"

"No!" Colt storms. "Just say it!"

"Is it green? It's green—"

"You already guessed green!"

"That was a different green! Dad, is it green? No, orange? Is it orange?"

Colt claps his hands to his face. He hears his mother laugh sympathetically, but her sympathy is useless, insulting, a leaf thrown into ocean. It is stuffy behind his hands, airless in the lounge room where the sun has shone through the big window all afternoon. The walls of the house are freshly painted in a shade of sand-dune beige, and smell like something plastic lifted out of a long-closed cardboard box. From the newly-laid carpet rises an odour of chemicals and glue. There had been a different smell when he'd seen the house for the first time, the day on which he'd been told it was to be his new home—a papery smell, like a wasps' nest, and the walls had been the palest blue. On the mantel had been arranged a picket-fence of keys, each attached by a short string to a cardboard label. *Front door spare, screen door original, side door, garage door, laundry overhead cupboard:* he'd never known a house in need of so many keys, as if each corner concealed a secret. His father had swept the keys and their cards into his jacket pocket. Colt has no need for keys: his mother doesn't work, so when her sons come home from school she is there; whatever she's done that day, she has finished doing. She has a car key, and a duplicate of the front-door key. All the other keys Colt has never seen again. At the mantel, their father is laughing. "Isn't that what postmen ride, orange bicycles? Do you want to be a postman, Bas?"

Bastian screws his face up merrily. "Dad! No!"

"If I gave you an orange bike, you might turn into a postman! Maybe that's how postmen become postmen?"

"Don't be silly!"

That's red bikes, Colt thinks into his hands: it's red bikes postmen ride, you . . . *moron.* Because on this night when truths are rising to the light, he's seeing this too: his father can be absurd. He's been a god and then a man of miracles and of late he has sometimes seemed a stranger to Colt, or someone he wishes were a stranger, but through all this downhill metamorphosing his father has remained a man of dignity: *absurd* comes to Colt like the scratch that makes the record player's needle skim. He lowers his hands to consider his father in this new, diffuse light. He's amazed that it's taken him so long to see it, and wonders how much else he is missing. The evening is warm, but Colt feels cool. As if to halt what he's thinking dead in its tracks, their mother finally speaks. "Dinner's almost ready, Rex."

And perhaps even their father is bored, as it must be boring being ringmaster to such witless clowns: "All right," he says, pushing away from the mantelpiece, "you can give up. It's an impossible task for two intelligent boys. Dinner's almost ready. Quick then, let's look at this bike."

It is parked outside, on the porch, below the lounge-room window. The four of them crowd around it like sheep at the manger, Bastian's hands fluttering to his mouth. The bike is a BMX, with wide chrome handlebars like a stag's horns, and vinyl-covered rolls of padding press-studded to the handlebars and frame. Its crow-dark tyres are densely, deeply knotted. The narrow seat is hardly present, not intended for sitting on; the handgrips are knobbly, the pedals serrated for grip. It has no gears, but its brake cables curve boldly, silver-threaded antennae. Not everyone has such a machine, they're a marvel seemingly just recently delivered into the world, and standing beside it Colt feels the warmth of its desirability. It smells of its newness, and in the entire world there is no better smell. But what he sees is the hook that was buried in his father's game, the treacherous seaweed beneath the waves; and in the moment when he should thank his father, what he says is, "It's black. I guessed black."

"It's charcoal," their father corrects. "What do you reckon, Bas?"

Bastian has the wide eyes of a fawn, the colour of caramel syrup.

There's a kind of trepidation in them now, an awe of how good life can get. "Oh Dad!" he breathes.

"Rex," says their mother, "you spoil them."

"Ah well!" Their father shrugs helplessly. "Why not? There's been a lot happening lately, new house, new school, but you've been good about it, haven't you, boys? You haven't complained. And what goes better with a new neighbourhood than a new bike to ride around on? All the kids will want a piece of this when they see it, won't they? The fellow in the shop said it's the kind all the boys want."

And Colt, who hadn't known complaining had been an option, runs his fingers over the BMX's shiny frame and perceives that this is why he — for it will be he, not Bastian, who commands this savage thing — now owns it, and owns so many good things, and only has to ask in order to receive more. Their father piles his sons with objects worth envying, so he will be the father of envied sons. Two boys, one bike: it's not for them, it's for him.

It is murky, this perception — he has a sense of something charmless shifting its position, something which sees him but which he is failing to see. He lets his hand drop. "Do you like it?" his father's asking.

"I love it," says Bastian heartily.

"It's great." Colt looks at his father, who is framed against the white sky and the last fanning rays of the light. "Thanks, Dad."

"Can we go for a ride, Dad?"

"We'll take it for a test-run after dinner," says Rex. "And there's the weekend ahead of you, remember. Plenty of time. Dinner first, fun later."

He spins his younger son around and smacks him on the tail, and Bastian, released from the spell of the marvellous thing, shoots into the house, flailing with excitement. There's the merest moment, as their father follows the boy inside, for Colt to catch his mother's eye. "I guessed black," he says. "Charcoal is black."

He sees her concede with the faintest of nods. "You've got it now," she says. "Don't make a fuss."

Freya Kiley has started to see things she hasn't seen before. Until recently she has lived as every child must: as someone dropped on a strangers' planet, forced to accept that these are the ways of this world. Being a child, she thinks waftily, is like being in rough but shallow water, buffeted, dunked, pushed this way and that. If it is sometimes alarming, there is always the sight of the beach. There's always the sand under your feet.

The problem, however, is that sand is sand. From where she sits she can almost feel it, the way the water sluices the grains away from heels and toes. It's stupid to put your trust in sand. And when you're a child, that is what you are: stupid.

When she was younger—nine, ten—Freya had tried to be holy. Piety was one of the rare things which the nuns at school approved of in a child; more than that, it seemed to be something she had no choice about. Certain traits characterised this world: the sun rose, dogs chased cats, and God lay underfoot everywhere like a clammy carpet. So Freya had tried to love the lamblike Jesus with his flowing hair, she'd strained to feel the presence of her guardian angel. She'd dwelt upon the cloudy Heaven awaiting her at the end of her hardly-begun life. If it had always been an effort, if her thoughts had repeatedly roamed, she'd assumed it was because religion was nerve-wracking. Talking snakes, toady plagues, corpses walking, people drinking blood. A mutilated man nailed to planks, his brow pierced by infectious-looking thorns. And, overseeing everything, a vile-tempered ghost, an emaciated and rebukeful old man in a hospital gown, watching and waiting to notch up a girl's smallest mistake. A God who was always harsh and rarely fair, who would hurl even an infant to Hell.

Now she's older and smarter, and she's starting to see that the world is a castle, and that a child lives in just one room of it. It's only as you grow up that you realise the castle is vast and has countless false floors and hidden doors and underground tunnels; and that the castle is haunted, and that the castle scares even itself. And as you get older, you're forced out of the room, whether you want to go or not. Freya wants, with urgency, to go.

Already, through the first doorway, she's discovered this: the reason the angels and Heaven and the old ghost have never stuck with her is not that they're nerve-wracking, but that they are not true.

There was no particular moment of realisation: it is more like something she was born knowing, and the knowledge has been slowly making its way like a splinter to the surface, and now it has finally arrived. It's come accompanied by a sense of shame and hurt, as if she has heard at last a snigger that's been skulking behind her back. Freya glances around, and sees plain faces. No one is laughing, yet she hears it.

She sits down, because the time has come to sit. When the priest has finished talking, she'll stand. Her fingernails carve crescents in the polished pine of the pew. "The heart is deceitful above all things, and desperately wicked," the priest says, reading from the Bible which is a great gilt-edged slab, a monster book full of monstering: when Freya looks at the congregation, it doesn't seem wicked to her. Wicked would be interesting, but everyone looks dull, half-asleep, slightly angry. Her brothers and sisters are kids, and they're not wicked, only irritating, and if God were here she would tell him that nobody has her permission to say nasty things about them. The church is recently built from cream brick and too much glass, so the air is thick and overheated. It has hard-wearing brown carpet and teal-blue trim. It is meant to be modern — the crucifix above the altar is made from beams of industrial steel, so intimidating that Jesus has absented himself — yet the priest is reading the same old lines from the same old book. Freya's nails dig into the pew as if she'd screw the place up and throw it away. *This is the last time,* she swears. She will never come here again. She is not going to tell herself lies, nor accept the lies of others. From now on, she will do things properly.

And when it is finally over, the priest bowing before the altar and trudging off with his duckling row of boys into the private room where girls are not welcome, the morning is done as if packed into an elderly person's wardrobe, but at least she is free to leave. Freya would like to sprint away kicking her heels like a pony, but that's not what can happen. The aisle clogs with parishioners and she gets hemmed in, has to worm through gaps while her siblings and mother disappear out the doors. Distance stretches like toffee, for a moment she thinks she will never reach fresh air: at the door she's caught in a blockage that has congealed in the hope of seeing the priest as if everyone hasn't seen him just minutes earlier and can't also see him in the milkbar buying cigarettes and see his underwear, too, if they so desire, hanging on the line in the yard of the presbytery, and it amazes her that with these signs they don't see he's just a human, a man of baggy elastic and bad habits, and by the time she's dodged and wriggled her way into the sunlight she feels scorched with contempt for every last living thing.

Only to find that her mother, too, has been snagged, and is stopped on the path beside the carpark with Marigold and Dorrie sagging beside her and Peter in his stroller arching his chest against the straps, and she's talking with an awkward smile to a man and a lady and two boys Freya has never seen before. The sun is warmer than when she'd last been under it, the heat drawing fumes from the bitumen; cars are reversing, people are standing about, children are beginning to cry. She tries to slip past unseen but her mother catches her — actually lunges sideways to grab her — and tells the strangers loudly and eagerly, as if only enthusiasm keeps her heart pumping, "This is another of my daughters, this is Freya."

"Another!" marvels the man. "Quite a tribe!"

"Oh, yes." Freya's mother shakes her head with a kind of amused hopelessness. "There's always another one coming."

Already, after ten seconds, it is unpleasant to be waylaid in the shadeless carpark, people slamming doors around them, starting the engines of cars. It is fumy, gritty, over-warm. Peter, having tested the strength of his bindings, has subsided in calculation: time starts ticking to the moment he'll start to scream. Freya smiles unendearingly. "Hello."

"Freya's the eldest," her mother tells the strangers. "She's—how old are you, Freya?"

"Twelve," she says. "You know."

"Hello, Freya," says the woman.

"Hello." She doesn't care that the word sounds booted out of her.

"After Freya there's Declan, then Sydney, but . . ." Elizabeth Kiley scans the crowd, "I can't see them."

"They're gone," says Marigold blandly.

"And who's this fine chap in the pusher?" asks the man.

"This is Peter. He's the baby. Well, he's nearly two."

Peter looks up beseechingly. "He's adorable," says the lady.

"He breaks my stuff," says Dorrie.

"That's what baby brothers do, don't they, Colt?" The man gestures at the boy beside him, who stands in pristine silence. "Colt is twelve, the same as you, Freya."

"Uh." She's already looked at this silent boy—he's taller than she is, and more beautiful—and looked swiftly away. "I'm nearly thirteen," she clarifies.

"I'm five," submits Dorrie.

"I'm seven," says Marigold.

The man, who is tall and quite conspicuously handsome, who looks like an action-movie actor and whose presence only makes sense if the carpark is in fact a movie set, smiles radiantly and says, "Well, we're delighted to meet you. I'm Rex Jenson, and this is my wife Tabby, and these are our sons Coltrane—Colt—and Bastian. We've moved into a house around the corner from you. It's so nice to meet new neighbours."

Freya and her mother smile as if they agree it is very nice; in truth such friendliness is disconcerting, a gust of too-strong wind. Freya has never been introduced to adults by their Christian names, and it's as startling as hearing a swear-word. "It must be exhausting, shifting house," says Elizabeth, grappling. "I don't think I could do it."

"Well, it's not easy," the man agrees. "Nothing worth doing is, is it? But it will be worth it. It doesn't hurt to shake your life up a bit. Change is always good."

"Oh, yes," says Elizabeth hazily. These people are too elegant, too assured: Freya knows they are making her mother nervous. She's shunting the pusher back and forth so Peter flops like a fish.

"It seems a lovely neighbourhood," says Tabby, the wife.

"Oh, it is," Elizabeth says, and flounders on: "A few palings get pulled off fences sometimes. Some kids were going around smashing letterboxes—remember that, Freya? When was that? People were waking up to find their letterboxes all over the footpath."

"Ages ago," says Freya.

"It was a while ago. A year or two ago."

"You get that kind of thing everywhere," says Rex. "It's usually just kids."

"Bad kids," says Dorrie.

"Kids letting off steam." Rex smiles. "Kids growing up. What's a letterbox? It's nothing. Something you can replace."

Freya and her family gape at him, this man so kind and cavalier that he could forgive an awful act of vandalism. Freya's been taught about forgiveness all her life, but she's never actually met anyone inclined to practise it. She glances at the sons, Coltrane and Bastian, who stand beside their mother as placid as giraffes. Their father's attitude must be wasted on them, they look incapable of committing any kind of crime. It is not possible to imagine them racing off to play the pinballs, which is undoubtedly what Freya's brothers have done. The Jenson boys look like they should be etched into stained-glass windows, Sebastian pierced with arrows, the arrogant child lecturing the learned men. And suddenly Freya feels overcome, unreasonably hot and testy. It's time to go, but they stand as if paralysed beneath the man's beneficent smile. Elizabeth asks, "What do you do, Rex?"

"I'm a dentist," he replies.

"Ook," squeaks Marigold, and Freya likewise shrinks. There's nothing worse than that sprawling chair, that tray of dainty tools.

"Our dentist gives us lollies," says Dorrie.

"He yelled at me for crying," says Marigold.

"People must talk to you about teeth all the time," says Elizabeth.

"I don't mind," Rex answers. "I like teeth."

"Mum's got false teeth," Dorrie informs him.

"Dorrie!" Elizabeth gags, but Freya notes that the man's expression does not alter even minutely, that he's deaf to anything someone doesn't want him to hear. Freya herself can't help smirking; glancing away, she meets the eye of the tall boy, Colt. He's a slighter version of his film-star father, with the same thick chestnut hair — a *mop* of hair, like the lush pelt of an animal — worn long around his face, the same cheekbones and eyebrows and perfect nose. The younger boy has the same mahogany curls but his face is like his mother's, a pink girly mouth, a small chiselled chin. Both have their father's amber eyes and olive skin. They are well-dressed but the sense of quality goes deep, as if they are burnished right to the bone. Dorrie's revelation has brought a smile to Colt's face — Freya's heart is just starting to be stirrable, and it stirs now. He's smiling to *her,* and no one else in the world knows it. It sets her cheeks on fire, makes her head feel as if it's not reliably where it used to be. She looks for help to the last cars moving past on slow-turning wheels, to the priest standing at the church doors with the remnants of the flock, his altar boys nowhere to be seen. There is nothing to do except flee. "I'm going home," she tells her mother. "Do you want me to take Peter?"

"I'll come!" says Marigold.

Elizabeth says, "We're all coming, we're leaving now —"

"I'm leaving *now,*" says Freya.

"Nice to meet you, Freya," says the man, the dentist, Rex Jenson. "Hopefully we'll see you again soon."

"Uh," says Freya. And almost runs.

The church isn't far from their home, which is the only good thing about it. Marigold skips to keep up with her sister, and the street streams past them as lines in the footpath, gates in fences, telephone poles planted in naturestrips. Jogging along, the girl tells Freya, "I liked that lady with a name like a cat."

"Tabby."

"Tabby." Marigold meows.

They pass a pole and a pole and another pole before Freya slows down. She wrinkles her nose, shakes her hair. "Those people were strange."

"How come?"

"Well. He talked and talked, but the lady hardly said anything, and those boys just . . . stood there."

"Rude?"

"Not rude," Freya judges. "Just strange."

Marigold flies her palm above the peaked top of a brick fence, thinking about this. She's young, but she is clever. "They were like those people in Mum's knitting magazines."

"Exactly!"

"Robots."

They have reached Freya's favourite house, which has a population of repellent concrete gnomes arranged in its front yard. Normally they'd slow or even stop, but Freya marches on. "Not robots. More like . . . aliens. Aliens trying to be humans."

"Creatures from the black lagoon," says Marigold, a movie fan.

"They wear skin to look like people, but they don't know how to *be* like people. They're learning it."

"Strange!" agrees Marigold. "Spooky."

"They *are* spooky. I mean, how did they know we live around the corner from them?"

"They saw us walking to church. That's what the man said, that they were walking behind us."

This is plausible, which is disappointing, but Freya's mind catches on the thought of Colt walking behind her, seeing her without her seeing him. She wishes she could go back in time to hover over that oblivious girl, tweak her hair, do something. She'd given Dorrie a cuff: knowing he must have seen it makes her feel harassed. "Well, why did they come here?" she asks hotly. "Dentists are rich. They make lots of money. So why are they here?"

Her sister is too young to have much concept of the wider world — Freya knows for sure that she thinks the starving Africans live near enough to have her leftovers delivered to them on a plate — and asks, "Where should they be?"

"Somewhere fancy! Where rich people live. Not here."

Marigold ponders. "Maybe they don't want to be fancy?"

"Everyone wants to be fancy."

"Maybe they're hiding."

Freya smiles, pleased by the idea of aliens hiding in a nondescript suburb, laying out their plans on a speckle-topped kitchen bench. In truth she admires strangeness, and likes the new neighbours for it. She strides along, ignoring her sister's scrabble to keep up, the air balmy as it weaves between her fingers, the sun a molten crown on her head. In a minute they'll be home — once they cross this road she will be able to see the white post-and-rail fence of their house. If her brother Declan were a friend of Colt Jenson's, he would bring him to the house sometimes. That's a fact, but Freya knows little about the friendships of boys, how they meld or repel. A stringy green weed pokes over the path and she plucks it as she passes, swishes it violently. "Well, who cares," she says, and doesn't answer when Marigold asks, "Who cares about what?" Instead she will think of what she does know, the sturdy posts in her life. The year is coming to its close: soon the long school holidays will begin, stretching past Christmas and into the new year when, returning to classrooms, she will be starting secondary school, the baby of the schoolyard but a baby no more. She'll be thirteen, a teenager, a creature of change. Already atheism sits inside her as comfortably as an egg in a nest. Next Sunday, when she refuses to go to church, her mother might rage, and to defend her position Freya will call upon the example of her father, which is something she would only do in an emergency and actually has never done before. And it will feel like a betrayal, using him against her mother. It *will be* a betrayal. The heart is wicked. Freya sighs.

They are within reach of their house — the spindly pine in the front yard, the clangy metal letterbox, the rut in the naturestrip where the station wagon cuts the corner; no sight makes her happier than the sight of home — when thoughts of her mother make Freya think of something else. She remembers Elizabeth saying, "There's always another one coming."

The words are written on one of the imaginary castle's innumerable doors, a warped and ponderous door which requires a mighty shove before it will open; but when it does, and when Freya sees what's behind it, the dismay dazes her.

Avery Price looks like a pixie found shifting through dandelions at the end of an overgrown garden; he should have wings jutting out his shoulderblades. He is small for his age and as translucently white as a pearl. Grey-eyed and fair-haired, with the pretty bowed lips of an infant, he is delicate, origami, he looks as if the only sustenance he requires is the occasional lettuce leaf sprinkled with sugar, and indeed he hardly eats anything more sustaining. Beneath the dainty façade, however, Avery is a wild child, the kind of boy-without-boundaries that other children enjoy having as a friend because there is nothing he will not do. He isn't a complainer or in any way a sissy—he's a smiler, a forgiver, there's no meanness in him. Despite this, it's evident that Avery is destined to follow a hard path through life—it's as obvious as the bruises, the unbrushed hair, the dirt-lined fingernails and the cheap, inadequate clothes. There's a sense that one shouldn't grow too fond of him. He's only eleven, and already the world is striving to be rid of him: when a dog rushes a fence and startles him into slipping off the gutter he's been stepping along, this most minor accident skins a great gouge from his knee, such an over-abundance of damage that Syd and Declan Kiley are stunned.

He's as tough as a boot, however. After hopping about on the road gasping, "Ow, ow," Avery sits on the kerb and inspects the wound with stoic curiosity. It's a gruesome thing, rag-edged, pipped with stones, as broad as a boy's palm. Crimson blood runs down his shin, crests his meatless calf and drips onto the road. Declan and Syd perch beside him, peering like scientists. "Bloody hell," says Declan.

"I think I see bone," says Syd.

Declan winces. "That is really disgusting."

"Shut up!" Syd screams at the dog, who's still barking.

Someone from the house calls the animal in, and silence returns as it always does to these streets. Occasionally music will float beyond a window, and on weekends there will be the odd lawnmower, a random car horn beeping farewell; but typically there is this silence, and the surreal sense of living on after the rest of existence has ceased. It's easy to believe the houses are empty, the occupants obliterated in some worldwide catastrophe, and that a boy like Syd Kiley can now rummage through strangers' cupboards at leisure. He can hardly imagine anything he'd enjoy more, being the last person alive, with access to all that stuff. Now he cocks his head to gaze into the depths of Avery's injury; this close he can smell a fleshiness, the taste of Avery raw. "Look at that. That's a piece of road."

They are a couple of blocks from Avery's home; Declan asks, "Can you walk? Do you want me to go and get your bike?"

"Or a wheelchair?" suggests Syd. "A walking-stick? We could bring Peter's pram."

"I'm OK," says Avery wanly. "I'll just stay here a minute."

"I really can see bone," says Syd.

The three boys sit back on the naturestrip, their feet in the gutter. Avery's sandals have thin soles and are slightly too small for him; by January, when summer has parched the grass into a crisp matting, the boys will be constantly stopping while Avery plucks prickles from his heels. Syd sits with his head bowed, the sunshine pressing firmly on the nape of his neck, thinking about this and about nothing. Between his own sandalled feet is a patch of bitumen, very grey and stony. With some work he assembles a wad of spit, and feeds it out as a sparkly thread. The thread breaks before it reaches the ground, marking the road with a dark spot shaped like a thorn. An interesting stone, clear like a diamond, catches his eye. He plucks it up and holds it above the gory swatch of Avery's wound. His brother and his victim watch in silence, Declan's blue eyes almost closed. Syd glances at Avery. "Dare me?"

"Go on," says Avery.

"I will," Syd threatens.

"I said do it," Avery replies.

So Syd lets the stone drop, and it lodges in the cushion of blood and must sting, because Avery gives a shuddery flinch. The boys watch as the stone topples painstakingly from its perch, lolling along a bloody rivulet before dropping to the road wearing a ruby cap. Syd sniffs, satisfied. Declan buries his face in his folded arms. There's a hoop of sunburn between his shoulders already.

There is no hurry to leave; they are headed nowhere. After a while Avery asks, "Are you going away for the holidays?"

"Mum hasn't said." Declan speaks into his knees. "Probably." Their mother always takes them somewhere, even if only for a week or two to a caravan park a few blocks back from the beach; on the weekend their father will drive down for the day and give the kids dolphin rides through the green water. Neither of the Kileys asks if Avery will likewise be going away. He is the child who haunts these streets, lurking in the places where pest species are found, the side door of the kiosk at the cricket ground, the bottle depot behind the Scouts' hall, the grassy veins of unowned land that divide houses here and there. It's possible he has never gone anywhere beyond the reach of his battered bicycle, and that he is obliged by the natural order to stay. If he were to leave, something would have gone wrong.

Syd feels a surge of impatience, shuffles his feet so his sandals chuff the road. He has no authority but he says, "Let's go."

Declan lifts his head and looks at Avery, who says, "Yep." But in the past minutes his knee has stiffened, and when he moves, he limps. He limps across the naturestrip to the footpath, hoisting and shuffling the damaged leg. It's an injury, Syd is wearied to see, which is going to take a long time to heal, which will glaze over and break open and glaze and break for days before it finally scabs, and the scab will crack and pull, and weep. It will be their damp companion all summer, they'll be witness to its entire lifespan. From the footpath Declan looks back at his brother. "You coming or not?"

Avery, too, has looked around, his bad leg posed on its toes. He freezes like that and says, "Oh, shit."

And then, with a rodent's instincts, he bolts: forgetting his pain he flees across the naturestrip and onto the open ground of the bitumen. The road sweeps downhill and around a broad corner, and Avery, following it, is gone like a dart shot from a blowpipe. Declan and Syd stand stupefied, staring after him. Then they look to see what their friend must have seen, and there's Garrick Greene lumbering toward them like a cannonball. And Declan says, "Ah, cods."

The boy arrives claret-faced and heaving—he's heavy-set and nuggety, not built for speed. His burning sights are on the spot where Avery was last seen, but he cannot take another step and thunders to a halt beside the brothers. "I'm gonna kill that prick," he gasps.

"What's he done?"

Garrick bends double, his hands on his knees, blowing like a bellows: Syd stares in revulsion at the flesh bunching at his neck. At school he's read a book about medieval farmers, and Garrick could have posed for the picture of the farmer's leather-aproned son. His limbs are weighty, over-stuffed, equal parts lard and muscle. His black hair is thin and floppy, groomed into greasy strings. His deep-set eyes are skidmarks left by the tyres of a crashing car. His hands are remindful of the vice bolted to a bench in the Kiley garage. Certain factors make Garrick Greene worth knowing—he sometimes has money, he has no respect for the law, he's as strong as he looks, and he looks like a bull—but to

Syd's mind these virtues are rarely reason enough. Garrick, however, is a neighbourhood boy, he comes with the territory and he's impossible to avoid: being his friend is smarter than not being his friend. He hasn't yet caught enough breath to speak, is huffing and puffing into his thighs, and Syd throws a jeering smile at Declan, who ignores it. Garrick heaves more, then straightens, swiping a wrist across wet lips. His gaze jumps around the brothers as if he's never seen them before. "He called my sister a bitch!"

Declan says, "What?"

"He called my sister a bitch!"

A yelp of laughter would escape Syd, but he wisely keeps it imprisoned. Garrick is the youngest of a large family, each member of which has a toe-curling reputation. The brothers can guess which of his many sisters is in question, a terrifying girl of sixteen who, wishing Declan to step aside at the milkbar counter one day, flicked her finger against his temple so hard it made him cry. She is either lying about the name-calling, or Avery has gone insane. The Kileys know that Garrick has no particular fondness for his sister, upon whom they have heard him bestow descriptions far worse than *bitch*—indeed, Garrick never shies from exposing much about his sister that the girl would presumably prefer to remain unpublicised. He tells them when a tampon has been fished out of the box and when she has a particularly gross pimple, he's shown them a love letter she had written, at the bottom of which the admired boy had printed, *Get lost mole.* He once stole a bra from her drawer and jiggled it in his friends' faces. "So what?" Avery had said urbanely. "I see bras on the clothesline every day."

And it is true that Avery has a sister too, a willowy, rarely-seen girl just as slatternly as Garrick's sister, but beautiful as a swan. Her bras would make laundry buckets of Garrick's sister's underwear. Garrick had jammed the garment into his pocket in silence and it was never seen again. Something creepy happened to it, Syd is sure.

Declan asks, "Why would he do that?"

"Who knows?" snarls Garrick. "What difference does it make?"

"He must have had a reason—"

"Who cares about a reason? He's not allowed to do it. But he did, and now he's gonna pay!"

Syd looks to his brother—his thoughtful, wily brother—and sees Declan considering the situation. It's important never to show fear with Garrick, he's told Syd that before. "You call her a bitch all the time," he says.

Garrick's eyes bulge, his hands fly. "That doesn't mean *he* can say it!"

It's an argument which makes sense to Declan and Syd, who come from a large and quarrelsome family themselves. The rules, they know, are different for insiders. Declan's blue eyes scan the treetops, the clouds, the silent houses on both sides of the road. "What are you going to do?"

"Teach him a lesson!" Garrick shouts. "Punch him in his smart mouth!"

The noise makes a bird whisk out of a tree, a dog bark from behind a closed door. Declan nods at the news. Somewhere in the world, Avery is still running; Syd pictures him lurching, exhausted, stumbling on, a trail of blood behind him, eyes spinning in his head. Either he will need to keep running forever, or this matter must be sorted. The boys live within streets of each other, their paths will cross for years. "Punch me," says Declan.

Syd swings to his brother. "Deco!"

"Huh?" says Garrick.

"Punch *me,*" says Declan again. "You've got to hit someone, so it might as well be me. Me—instead of Avery."

Garrick takes a leery step back from madness. "Nah, it doesn't work like that."

"Yeah it does—why doesn't it? A punch is a punch."

Garrick stares, his tongue probing his lips, and then he shakes his head. "I'm not gonna hit you, Declan."

"Why not?" Declan lifts his chin. "She *is* a bitch, your sister. I call her a bitch every day. Every time I see her, I say, *There goes that bitch.*"

"Shut up, Deco!"

"She should get it tattooed on her forehead: *I'm a big fat bitch.*"

Garrick is smiling, but his mouth is crooked. "I know what you're doing, Declan—"

"I'm telling you she's a bitch—"

"You're an idiot—"

"So punch me instead."

"Deco!"

"If you want me to, I will."

"Go ahead. Stop talking and do it."

"If you don't shut up, I'm going to."

"I'm telling you to do it!"

Garrick throws his arms out. "You want me to? You really really want me to?"

"Declan!" wails Syd, but the two older boys ignore him. Garrick assesses Declan, who stands casually, a cowboy, hands open at his sides. He is finely-made and lean, not tall, no competition for Garrick, except that he's a million times cleverer and more admirable. "I could punch you in the stomach," Garrick offers.

Syd bleats, but Declan says, "Then we'll be even, right?"

"Yeah," says Garrick, "I guess": then abruptly he's reneging, as if another personality has stepped in just as an unfair deal was about to be sealed. "Nah—I'll hit you, but I'll still want to hit *him*. I'll have to do it, Deco."

A look of disgust crosses Declan's face, and he turns away as if from a waste of his precious time, and Syd's heart bounds joyously—and Garrick says, "OK, OK, I promise! I won't hit the little shit as well. Jeez, Deco."

Declan turns to face him. "All right, do it."

"It's a pretty shitty deal, though. I was looking forward to bashing that turd."

"Do it or don't do it," says Declan coolly. "I'm not waiting around here all day."

"Deco!" Syd protests, but as usual he is ignored: Garrick rolls his shoulders, Declan plants his feet, and Syd watches in disbelief as the bigger boy steps forward and drives a fist into his brother's guts. Contact makes a thick, dire, deadened sound: Declan clutches his stomach and bends like a bow. Syd stares a moment, his mouth dropped open: then he leaps like a mongoose at Garrick, spangling with fury. "You shithead!" he screams. "You prick! You arsehole! You ape!"

Garrick swats him aside with hardly a glance, studying his victim, who is bent double with his arms clenched round his body. "Shut up, Syd," Declan croaks through gritted teeth. Garrick and Syd watch as he recovers, wincing and coughing and swearing and unfolding cautiously until he is standing straight, then wiping his eyes and pushing back his brown fringe and smiling gingerly, with relief. "Phew," he says, and chuckles.

Garrick asks, "All right?"

"Yeah, good."

Syd turns on Garrick. "You didn't have to hit him so hard!"

"I could of hit him harder."

"Forget it, Syd . . ."

"Yeah," Garrick tells the boy, "do what your brother says. It's done. The little weed survives another day." And because he does in fact like and respect Declan, he says, "You sure you're all right?"

Declan nods loosely. "You throw a nice punch."

"Yeah, but you're pretty tough," Garrick replies graciously.

The three boys loiter on the footpath, their shadows ironed behind them, the problem dealt with and already history for Garrick and Declan but never for Syd, who stores it in the chest of many grievances he keeps unlocked inside his head. "What do you wanna do?" asks Garrick; and Syd, who would rather that he and his brother went one way and the oaf went another, preferably to his death, nevertheless accepts in silence the bigger boy's attaching of himself to them, and looks on the bright side. Garrick might have money; there's a chance Garrick might be talked into doing something that will get him sent to a children's home. "Where were you going?"

Declan lies and says, "Nowhere."

"Wanna go to the stormwater?"

"Yeah." Declan looks at Syd. "You don't have to come."

"I'll come," says Syd.

Walking away, Garrick pokes a thick finger into Syd's spine. "Hey," he says. "Tiny-dick. Call me a shithead again, I'll knock your block off."

Syd stays lordishly silent, as if he's heard and felt nothing; but inside his head he tends the chest of grievances, in which there's plenty of room.

In the space between the garage and the back fence is a high pile of branches and pulled weeds, stashed there out of sight until the next time Freya's father can be bothered lighting the oil-barrel incinerator. Freya sometimes comes here, like a cat, in search of mice she never finds, and because it is one of the few places around the house where she can find solitude. No one except herself, as far as she knows, comes here with any frequency. No one else, as far as she can tell, hankers for privacy with the fretful, ceaseless restlessness that she does. So the wasteland behind the garage is her special alone place, but conveniently it's not so disconnected from the house that she can't sense what's going on in there. She's available to spring into action whenever the tyrannical command of an eldest child is required. Her siblings all fear her, even Declan: that's as it should be, as it needs to be. Crouching among the pikes of branches and the swags of parched leaves, she's telepathically aware of Dorrie raiding the kitchen in search of sugar, which she will spoon into her mouth as white mountains on a teaspoon; of Peter zooming down the hall on the wheeled walking-frame he has outgrown; of Marigold in the lounge room, sighing and sniffing over her homework; of the absence of Syd and Declan, who seize any opportunity to be away from the house. She senses her mother, nearby but distant, maybe in the front garden. Her father is beyond the reach of her powers. She's never been able to imagine where he spends his time.

The television is off. There is nothing in the oven. Across the kitchen table is spread a rattle of colouring pencils. The washing machine is churning through another load, its third for the day, because sunshine should not be wasted. Already the line is crowded with clothes, from Peter's stubby socks to Marigold's ladybird nightie to the workshirts of her father spread like wide blue wings. Even so, there's a hillock of garments growing stale beside the machine.

The Kiley house is a white weatherboard with black guttering and a red tile roof. Its floor plan is simple, its construction of mediocre quality. The land on which it stands is spacious without being generous. There is a big garage and a smallish shed, both made from fracturous fibro. The house is one of countless similar properties in the neighbourhood, not aged but growing tired, the trees in the yards and surrounding streets just reaching their full height. Freya's father, Joe, had bought the house only a couple of months before Freya was born — it's a piece of family lore, how Elizabeth had worried that they wouldn't have a proper home for the first baby. More lore is this: that Joe had wanted to buy a house miles away, on the outskirts of the city, practically in the country. Elizabeth recounts it like a horror story, but Freya thinks she might have liked living in the wild. She could have owned a pony. She might not have had to retreat, for seclusion, to the airless shadow of the garage.

When there had been only her parents and herself, the white house must have been roomy: there are three bedrooms, and Elizabeth says they made a nursery of the dinky middle room. The third room was for sewing, for books, for nothing. But then Declan was born and then Syd, then Marigold and Dorrie and Peter, siblings arriving like jetsam, like kittens to a barn, and now the three girls share the third room, and the older boys have the middle one. Peter sleeps in his parents' room, in a cot he's already too big for, but the middle room is too small to hold him and his countless accoutrements. Even the sisters' bedroom isn't large—Marigold and Dorrie must sleep in a bunk. The little girls don't mind sharing, they don't complain if Freya keeps her radio or reading-lamp on. They try to follow the rules of the room laid down by their dominant sibling. Nevertheless their clothes drift, their toys spill, their knick-knacks and crusts and shoes and ribbons and xylophones and schoolbags and books and hairbrushes and Barbies and Barbie clothes and Barbie shoes and naked Kens and homework and nail-clippings and drawings and tissues and hand-puppets and plastic jewels and sandwiches and singlets and chewy-wrappers and glass horses and bangles and hair-ties and teddy bears and pencils and cordial bottles and so much, much more clutters every surface and crowds across the floor. Regularly Freya flies into a rage over this mess and the extended mess, the mess which finds its way through the house like the ratty hem of a juvenile junkyard. Yet when she implores her mother to tell Syd, Marigold and Dorrie to tidy up after themselves, Elizabeth always answers, "Why? They'll just make more mess tomorrow." Which is the most infuriating and not-funny argument Freya has ever heard. In the past she's tried to enlist Declan to help enforce neatness on their siblings, but Declan, who owns the least of any of them, looked at her pityingly and said, "It's only stuff." He never seems to worry about anything that keeps Freya awake.

Mostly she worries about money, and the family's lack of it. The Kileys are not starving, and certainly not bleakly poor: but the tightness is always there, blandening the taste of things, sucking vibrancy out of the air. Everything a child might want is inevitably deemed too expensive to be purchased on a whim, from an ice-cream cake to a tin of Derwent pencils to a proper pair of Levi's with the patch-of-leather brand. Such luxuries must be reserved for special events, birthdays or Christmas, or they must be arduously saved for with pocket money. Freya's pocket money, received each Friday afternoon, buys, each Saturday morning, enough caramel buds to last the journey home from the shop.

The children look forward to Thursday, which is supermarket day; preserved in their collective memories are those occasions when there's been a jam log for them to chop up. Their hearts beat hard each shopping day, they pour through the front door. Usually, they are met with disappointment. Usually the haul consists of staples: white bread, oranges, sausages, potatoes. There have been days when the sight of these has so dispirited Freya that she's run to her hiding-place and cried. The only time they eat takeaway is when their father brings home a parcel of fish and chips. The children flock to the feast like bare-legged vultures, endure patiently Joe's ramshackle divvying of the meal. If they're lucky he will also have brought home a bag of Jaffas, which are not the children's favourite but are gobbled anyway. The younger children love these evenings, but lately they have been sticking in Freya's craw. Joe only buys fish and chips when he comes home late, rheumy-eyed and smelling of smoke, drawling his words and hungry. He spends whatever change he finds in his pockets and orders without thought, so there are never enough dim sims for everyone to have one to themselves, never enough fish for more than a bite or two. He wastes money on scallops, which everybody hates except he. All the vultures will get something, but it won't necessarily be what they'd prefer. Their mother will eat nothing, she and the children having already had their dinner of chops and potato, a plate of which had been set aside on the kitchen table for Joe. Now that meal will go into the fridge, to be eaten by Joe for breakfast, or by nobody. The children won't whine about their father's bounty, as they'd complained about their mother's. Elizabeth's resentment of all this won't go unnoticed by her husband, and beyond waste and guilt and unfairness and greed, this is what the feasts have come to represent to Freya: the simmering lack of love between her father and her mother.

It's taken a long time for her to recognise that her parents hate one another. For most of her life she's never given the situation any thought. The world was one way and, right or wrong, that was the only way it would be, and it simply never occurred to her that it could be another way. But now she is stepping through the amazing castle and she's beginning to see that life is much more intricate than she'd realised. Everything is part of a chain, each link locked in place by all the other links. Everything that happens is shaped by what's already happened, and shapes what is to come. Her mother and father haven't been her parents since time immemorial. They must have met at some point when they were younger, strangers, before their children were born, and they must have loved each other then, because only love would make them marry. She has seen the black-and-white wedding photographs, and both Elizabeth and Joe are smiling. In one of the photos Joe has his arm around Elizabeth's waist, which is something Freya can't imagine him doing. They never touch now — she's never seen them kiss. Since that smiling, black-and-white day, something has surely gone wrong. Maybe things go wrong for everyone — maybe all grown people are unhappy in the way her parents are, or maybe just the married ones, or maybe just the ones with children, she doesn't know. Maybe it's not even wrong, this mysterious metamorphosis — maybe this is how it is meant to be. All she knows for certain is that in the wedding photographs her mother and father seem happy, but that's not how they seem anymore.

Freya is hunched against the fence, squeezed into a gritty space between lopped branches of the plum tree. Although the garage shade falls across her, it's oppressively hot. She isn't unwell, but she feels she should be. Strands of long hair are sticking to her throat, her eyes are as dry as eggshells. It's uncomfortable and lonely but she feels driven here, penned into a last place of dubious safety.

"It's a pipe at the creek. You can walk inside it."

"It's good," says Avery. "It's scary."

There is a moment in which all the boys look down. Then, "You can come if you want," Declan tells Colt and Bastian.

Bastian says immediately, "I don't want to go somewhere scary."

"It's not really scary," says Avery.

"It's scary if you're a baby," says Garrick.

"No no," whines the child, "I don't want to go."

Declan looks at Colt. "What about you?"

"Yeah." The boy steps from the fence—he's taller than Declan, taller than Garrick. "I'll come."

"You shouldn't go, Avery," the man tells his patient. "A stormwater drain isn't a healthy place. If a bad bug gets into an open wound like yours, you could end up losing your leg. You can wait here, if you like, and Bastian can show you the toys. An absolute mountain range of toys, these boys have."

Garrick says, "Toys like what?"

"Oh, everything—you name it, they've got it! Skateboards, miniature trains, remote-control boats, who knows what else. It's probably time someone set up the track for the slot cars, isn't it?"

"I can do it," says Avery.

"And soon, in a week or so, there'll be something even better than slot cars, won't there, Bas?"

"Don't tell!" Bastian squeaks. "It's a super secret!"

"A super secret?" The man widens his eyes, which are a strange colour, Syd notes, like the sap where prehistoric beetles are drowned. "If you say so. But I don't think it can be a secret for long."

There's another pause; the neighbourhood ruffians shift their feet. No matter what else they are, they are children — a mountain range of toys gleams in their minds. And maybe the man knows it, because he says, "Why don't you all stay? It's a hot afternoon to be messing about in a creek. Look, you're already sunburned. I think there are icy-poles in the freezer, aren't there, Bas?"

"Pineapple ones," says Bastian.

Colt looks down at his father, who is still kneeling on the footpath. To Syd's mind Colt has the option of saying yes or saying no, but he looks as if the choice is more difficult. "Bring your friends in," his father tells him, squinting against the bright sun. "Get the trains and cars out. Don't leave your brother behind so soon. There's always another day for a stormwater drain."

Colt is silent. Then he turns to Declan, Syd, Garrick. "We can stay here," he says flatly, and not in the least as if they'd be welcome. But the man is rising, skyscraper tall, extending a hand to Avery, who's never been helped to his feet in his life. Garrick spins the dark nose of the BMX toward the house, and Syd, who wants so much that life might not give him, says, "I want a skateboard."

The red-brick house is a stranger to Colt: it's less than a fortnight since the family moved in, and he still feels like a visitor. Despite the new carpet and the repainting, the house stubbornly belongs to the person who used to live here: an elderly lady, his mother has told him, who'd become frail. She left a garden that is unusual for this neighbourhood, where most of the trees are self-sown oaks and ash, massive things which shade the yards and parch the lawns. The Jensons have inherited a garden of native brush and eucalypts, wispy and whippy, intriguingly untame. Bastian has found a bird feeder, there's a maze of stepping-stones, and in one tree is a wooden case made for sheltering possums. The house itself is spruce, the gutters clear, the hinges oiled, the flywire tight to the windows. In his bed at night—his own familiar bed, brought from their previous house—Colt thinks about the old woman, how she probably did not want to leave her stepping-stones and sleeping possums and her hand-planted trees. She must have left as heartsore as he had arrived. This is only the second house he's ever lived in, there's nothing to say his family will move from here, and surely it's just the dislocation making him think this way: but he pictures them packing again and again, driven on relentlessly. The ringing of the doorbell, the sour adult faces, the conversations behind doors. The boxing up of all they own, the strange keys on the mantelpiece, the gifting of new possessions. "Just leave it there," he tells Garrick of the BMX: leave the hateful thing where it falls.

Colt and Bastian each has his own bedroom — they have never had to share. Heading down the hallway they stop first at Bastian's door, and the boy flings into the room and bounces on the bed. For all his fussiness he is an untidy child, his bed unmade, his books piled in jutting stacks, the wardrobe door hanging open so some shoes are tilting out. His countless *Star Wars* people are strewn across the floor, mixed in with their weapons and spacecraft and puggy beasts as well as with Bastian's extensive fleet of Matchbox cars, all these small things combining to make an arena more vicious, to the bare foot, than a bull-ants' nest. "This is my favourite, Jawa," Bastian says, retrieving from the prone population a tiny figure and holding it up glowingly for their appreciation and envy. Bastian is vague, flighty, a puff of air; to Colt he is a cause for concern. He wishes his brother had been born a girl, a little lady content to be at their mother's side. It's too hard on Bastian to be a boy, there's no place for boys like him. He holds out the Jawa and the visitors stare as if he's mad, as if they'd bite their fingers off before touching that fawned-upon toy. And the awful thing is that Bastian doesn't notice, his happiness doesn't falter, he keeps smiling his foolish smile. "Come on," Colt urges, and

Bastian cries, "Wait!" because they've hardly spared his treasures even a minute of their time; but as they walk away he's with them, chirping and fluttering, a territorial bird.

Colt's room is organised: he could not have rested until it was so. It's a larger room than Bastian's, and the boys fan out within it. Mostly Colt owns books, a library ranged neatly across dustless shelves. Captured between the volumes is a gang of golden children frozen in positions of dash atop plinths inset with engraved plates. There are gilded cups, frilly rosettes, shield-shaped plaques, curling ribbons, metal medallions. Declan steps closer to read the words etched into the plates. "You're a runner?"

Colt shrugs modestly, but it's obvious he runs like the wind. There are some silvers and bronzes, token splashes of red and yellow as if to acknowledge that nobody is perfect, but the collection has its basis in gold and blue. *First, fastest, champion:* before they'd shifted to this house, into this world where he knows no one, Colt's closest friends, the ones with whom he'd had most in common, had been boys from the local athletics club. They would visit his bedroom and peruse the trophies just as Declan is doing, shifting through them as other boys shuffle football cards, reliving each moment of each race, quoting times to the millisecond. On Saturdays when he wasn't working the weekend shift at the surgery, Colt's father would watch the meets, and sometimes drive three or four of Colt's friends home afterwards. Usually he would detour to the bakery and buy softdrink and pies which the boys would eat around the Jensons' kitchen table, thin arms poking from their flimsy singlets, socked feet hooking the bars of the chairs. He'll never see any of those boys again, Colt knows. "I used to be," he tells Declan. "I'm not sure if I'll do it anymore. I was in a club, but — it's a long way from here."

"We lived miles and miles away," Bastian explains. "But not in another country."

"There must be an athletics club round here," says Declan, and frowns at Avery and Garrick. "Isn't there?"

"Avery should know," says Garrick. "He's always running."

"I probably won't do it anymore," says Colt.

Books and trophies are not what was promised, and Garrick blows air dismissively. "Where's all the good stuff? Where's the slot cars?"

Bastian hops excitedly from foot to foot; Colt knows he wants to clutch the big boy's arm the way he might want to carry the leash of a dog, but doesn't dare. "This way, hurry, I'll show you."

At the end of the hallway, tucked behind the kitchen, is a slope-ceilinged, sunlit room with a long row of louvred windows that look out over the rear garden. The old owner of the house probably read or dozed in here, Colt imagines: it was a room for peace. Until this minute, peace has reigned. "Bloody hell," says Garrick at the doorway.

His parents call it a *playroom,* but that's a word Colt would rather choke on than use. There'd been a similar room in their other house and, as children, he and Bastian had played in that one. But at some point their father had begun to buy his sons everything they wanted and so much they didn't ask for as well, and the room and its contents became less about playing and more about owning in abundance things which others wish for and do not have. And as the boys crowd at the door catching their breath in amazement, Colt sees it all, suddenly, for what it is. His father spends money not merely on making his sons envied, but on making them—and the word seems to tip the floor—*enticing*. His father buys bait. And Colt is engulfed with such disorienting shame that he has to move away quickly, striding the length of the room as if he's spotted something about to topple. In the corner there's a basket of tennis balls capped by the greater orb of a soccer ball, which he picks up and holds stupidly, having no idea what to do with it, having never played soccer in his life. He looks back over the distance he's travelled—past the cricket bats and tennis racquets and boxes of Monopoly, Scrabble, Cluedo, Operation and KerPlunk; past the footballs lolling against the skirtingboard, all of them scarcely-scuffed Sherrins; past the record player with its twin mesh-fronted speakers, the podgy vinyl beanbags slouched on the floor—and his heart is beating like it must burst. There are a trillion pieces of Lego and Meccano, model cars and aeroplanes and tanks in packages yet to be opened. There are plastic soldiers in their hundreds flung into a bucket grave, and fine painted lead ones preserved in velvet-lined trays. There is a wad of larger warriors, G.I. Joes in ill-fitting camouflage, and a pair of Six Million Dollar Mans with tunnels drilled starkly through their manly heads. There's a miniature train in countless pieces, the assembling of which will require a weekend of work. There are radio-controlled vehicles of various makes and sizes. There is the slot-car set, bought from a specialist store and lifted down from the highest shelf. They had had difficulty fitting the box into their father's car. In all this trove, not one thing is broken or outmoded, no parts are loose or lost: Colt knows that every puzzle possesses its exactly required number of pieces. The textas in their plastic slips are not running low on ink. Anything that feeds off batteries is dutifully fitted with them. And if by some strange intrusion of harsh reality something happens here as it happens elsewhere—something snaps, drops off, wears away, if the punching clown is punctured or the player starts chewing up tapes—then that broken thing is not repaired or driven, lamed, into further service, but thrown away like a disgusting thing, and replaced by a flawless example of its kind.

It's less a playroom, Colt thinks, than a place which trills with nerves.

"Oh, this is ace." All the cynicism that keeps Garrick motoring has fallen away. "Oh, this is really ace."

"Look, look!" Bastian pushes past, dashes randomly around the room. He picks up a wooden case and proffers it to Avery: "Look, a microscope!"

Syd walks to where the skateboards stand wheels-up against the wall, crouches before them and turns them over as reverently as if they were infants in their cradles, the broad red-and-white striped one, its sleeker jewel-blue pair. The slot cars have caught Garrick's eye and he seizes the great box with both hands, wrestling it away from the wall. "Where can we set it up?" he wants to know, and Bastian starts booting the beanbags aside, piping, "Here, I'll help you, Colt and me will help!" And Colt will help, but first he must fight down the urge to order them out of the room, out of the house, away from the whole street, he'd close up this room like a pharaoh's cursed tomb until the toys had crumbled away. His heart is still pounding, he feels he's turned grey, and he goes to the window as if something unusual out there has caught his eye. A warm breeze slides between the louvres, scurfs locks of hair across his forehead. His fingers dig into his palms, and he commands himself not to panic. He can't hear them, but he's aware of his parents in the house somewhere, his father speaking in his nothing-ever-goes-wrong voice, his mother answering with murmurs which quieten into smiles and then into nothing.

The back garden is a sparse forest of rocks and scrub and eucalypts. Some of the trees close to the deck have been daubed with yellow paint: these are the ones with only a day or two left to stand. When they and the scrub around them have been grubbed away, a clearing will be opened in the yard, and from this window the view across it will be excellent. By this time next week, give or take a couple of days, the clearing will be occupied by a swimming pool. Not an extravagant, sunken pool—merely the above-ground, fibreglass-walled kind, which isn't as fancy but is quicker to install and which will still be impressively large and deep. A swimming pool of their very own: Bastian's super secret, impossible to keep.

Wednesday is payday, and at the printworks the men are paid in cash; it's a great temptation, that fold of bills, and it's a tradition for the men to finish Wednesday evening at the nearby hotel. They set themselves no limit to how much of their wage they may spend, but if they are smart they will first tuck, into an unpillageable pocket, the amount required by their wives for the housekeeping. Not all the men are smart, and even the clever ones aren't consistently clever, but Joe Kiley usually manages to bring home and place on the kitchen table the thin pile of notes which must keep his family through the coming week. His daughter Freya sees the money with relief. There have been times when her father has been light-fingeredly separated from his earnings, and he's been as sullen about it, at home, as if one of his children were to blame. But tonight the money is there, and Freya gathers it up when Joe turns to the refrigerator. She knows he's been drinking. "How was work?" she asks, but he doesn't hear. She is holding her breath but even when she tries to relax and breathe properly, she can't do it. "Your dinner's in the oven," she tells him; she's told him this already, but Joe says,

"You could have told me, Frey," and swings the fridge door closed. As he retrieves the plate from the oven she sees he's sporting a mean black cut across his left thumb: the printworks is a dangerous place, men have lost fingers to the razoring machines. A tiny part of her is permanently given over to dread of such an accident befalling her father. It would tear her heart to pieces, she thinks.

She slips from her chair and goes into the lounge, where the rest of her family are watching television. Anyone looking through the wide window would see a woman at ease with her children, because Dorrie and Marigold are sprawled on the floor, their faces tipped to the TV, and Peter is lying between them feeding plastic animals into a shoebox, and Syd is curled in one armchair and Declan is lying loosely across the other, and their mother is standing at the table folding the washing but following what's happening on the screen. The watcher beyond the window wouldn't know how closely they are listening to the man in the other room—the peeling back of the foil from the plate, the opening and banging closed of the sticky cutlery drawer. The watcher wouldn't feel the thinning of the air.

Freya gives her mother the housekeeping money, and Elizabeth says, "Oh, thanks," so casually, as if it doesn't mean much to have those notes closed in her hand. Freya would help her fold the washing but the basket is nearly empty, its contents transformed into a small township over the table. Each pile has its destination: the linen press, the tea-towel drawer, the hallway cupboard, the inadequate chests in the children's bedrooms. She hasn't asked her mother about any baby that may or may not be on its way—it's a tricky subject to approach, mortifying in the deadliest way—but Freya thinks of the clutter a baby brings with it, the nappies, the bibs, the cloths for sponging the ceaseless purge. The township of clothes is already crowded, the table simply not broad enough for another inhabitant to exist there.

She sits on the couch, separated by the telephone stand from Syd in his armchair. Syd is small and as neatly-made as a cat, cat-faced with his wide blue eyes and small nose and whiskery hair, and he curls on the chair like a cat, his temple on the padded arm, his hands woven under his chin. There's a noise from the kitchen—a knife dropped onto the floor—and his feet in their droopy socks flex. Moments pass and there's another noise, their father's chair dragged on the lino: like a cat's tail twitching, Syd's feet churn again. Across the room, Declan's gaze is unflinchingly on the screen. There are glass doors set into the lounge-room window, they open onto the veranda and the front yard and freedom; they are open now, and the air comes in, lifting the pages of Marigold's schoolbook. It's early evening but the sky is light, the clocks having been pushed forward for daylight saving. Only the faintest haze of evening stains the clouds milk-grey.

They hear the shoving of his chair, his tread across the kitchen.

Her father is not a big man, but he's the biggest person in the house: he seems to fill the lounge-room doorway right up to the top of the frame. Marigold and Dorrie lift their heads like flowers. "Hi, Dad," says Dorrie.

"Hi, girls. Hello, Peter. Hello, Sydney. Hello Declan. Hello Elizabeth."

"Hello, Joe," says Freya's mother.

He slaps his thigh. "Come here, Petey-boy, give me a kiss."

Peter's silky head sinks, and Marigold says, "He's busy, Dad. He's playing with his animals."

Joe comes into the room: he's not unsteady, but they can see it and smell it, the glasses he's drained, the foam on the glass. A Christmas card stands on the sideboard and he pinches it up, peers into its depths. "Who are Joan and Jack?"

"Next door to my parents."

"Who?"

"The people who live next door to Mum and Dad." Elizabeth sighs as if every word is pain, and the children are quiet because they can hear it, everything that is coming.

Joe pouts. "Isn't it—November? That's not Christmas. In a hurry, are they? Think it might be their last one?"

Freya chuckles obligingly, but Elizabeth says nothing. "Funny people to send a Christmas card," Joe decides. "We don't even know them."

"I do."

"What?"

"I know them." Their mother's voice is an ice floe. The folding is done and she's jamming the piles in the basket, and Freya wants to beg, *Please, Mum.* There is no point being angry. It makes things worse and he never seems to care.

Joe sets the greeting-card down, moves further into the room. "What are you watching, kids?"

Everyone waits for somebody else to answer. "Just a dumb show," says Marigold.

"If it's dumb, why are you watching? What's it about?"

None of his offspring look away from the screen, on which people in drab clothes are grouped in a cold-looking kitchen. "Just stuff," says Marigold vaguely.

"Stuff? What is stuff?"

"It's a serial," says Syd.

Joe says, "A serial killer," and Freya laughs again. She, like all Joe's children, has inherited his blue eyes and fly-away fisherman's hair, his pale skin and lightly-made frame. None of them have their mother's farm-girl colouring or sturdy build; they cleave to her, but belong to him. "What's it about?" he asks again.

"For God's sake, Joe!" says Elizabeth. "Let them watch in peace."

But there can't be peace, not now. "It's about these people," says Syd. "It's hard to explain. You haven't been watching it—"

"Doesn't matter if I've been watching it or not. You've been watching, and I'm asking you."

"Leave them alone!" says Elizabeth, and Freya feels everything sliding.

"It's about people in the war." Declan speaks curtly, without looking up. "It's boring, Dad."

"It's boring, yet you're all sitting there like monkeys staring at it. Turn off the TV and I'll tell you a story. Would you like that, Dorrie doll?"

"Yeah!" Dorrie scrambles to her knees.

"When the show's finished, Dad," Syd groans. "Sit down, Dorrie, your head's in the way . . ."

"Turn it up," says Declan, and Marigold crawls over her book to twist the volume knob. Joe makes a sound which suggests his children disappoint him. Elizabeth has stacked the basket and the stack is precarious, but she doesn't carry it away. Leaning on the back of Declan's chair Joe observes the program in silence, and no one else says anything, so Freya hears it clearly above the yawing of the television: the low hum that is their wish that he would leave. She wishes they could be glad he's here—it's what he would like, it's what any child would choose—but it has never been that way, and it tests her imagination to believe any other way exists. "Hey," says Joe, and the pressure is a hand pushing down on Freya's chest. "Hey girls, Petey, let's set up the Christmas tree."

This catches the attention of the youngest ones: Marigold looks up with interest, and Peter says, "OK!"

"No," says Elizabeth, "not tonight."

"Mum!" cries Dorrie.

"You're having a bath when the show's finished."

"I don't want a bath!" The little girl is instantly on the edge of hysteria. "I want to set up the Christmas tree!"

Freya finds herself speaking. "It's too early for the tree, Dorrie. It's a long time until Christmas. All the decorations will fall off and get broken."

"We've already got a Christmas card," Joe points out.

"They won't get broken, Freya!"

"Turn up the TV," murmurs Declan.

"Mum said you can't—"

"Dad says I can! I want to! I want to!" And Dorrie throws back her head and bawls.

"Turn up the TV!" Declan hisses.

"Don't, Marigold!" barks Freya.

Elizabeth says, "For God's sake, Joe, why don't you go to bed?"

Marigold rounds on her sister and thumps her, shrieking, "Shut up, you stupid idiot!"

"I want to set up the Christmas tree!" howls the child; and Peter, in the crossfire, slumps to the carpet and weeps.

"Look what you've done, Dad!" cries Syd. "We were trying to watch TV!"

"She wants to set up the Christmas tree!" Joe laughs like he's innocent and amazed. "That's not too much to ask, is it?"

He flops on the couch beside Freya, seeming to forget, as he does so, all about Christmas and his traumatised children. Over the storming of their grief he asks her, "What's happening on this show?"

"Dad!"

"All right, all right! Don't tell me."

He settles into the couch and closes his eyes, and the outcome of the evening wheels like a compass needle. A smell rises from him, broken glass, stained tiles, ashtrays, ill-care, the worst smell the children know. Marigold turns the volume down, and, "Stop crying!" Declan snarls at Dorrie and Peter, who struggle to gulp down their misery, chests jerking, faces drenched.

Freya glances at her father's pockets, where money sometimes falls out.

Then he opens his sea-blue eyes and the first thing he sees is Declan, lying with his legs hanging over the arm of the chair.

"Sit up," he says unpleasantly, in a voice that is and isn't his own. "A chair's for sitting on. Not sprawling all over like a dog."

"Oh, shut up." The words sound as if Elizabeth has breathed them from glowing coals. Her husband, if he heard, disregards her, watching sourly as Declan shuffles upright. "About time you were in bed, isn't it?" he says. "There's school tomorrow."

"Leave him alone," says Elizabeth. "Don't start, Joe—"

"School tomorrow, Declan." Joe jerks his chin. "Time to get to bed."

Declan does not look at his father, stares fixedly at the TV. Its images change every few seconds; nothing else does. When he doesn't move, their father says more fiercely, "Declan, what did I just tell you?"

"Dad," says Freya quietly, "it's not even dark."

But they know what he's like. He's a recording of something dreadful, which loops and starts again. "Declan Kiley. Get to your room. I will not tell you a second time."

Elizabeth snaps, "Why don't *you* get to *your* room! No one wants to listen to you!"

He turns his face to her, a blotched mask recognisable only because they've seen it before. There is no kindness in it. Before anything else can happen, Declan gets to his feet. And this is new—usually his father's chivvying drives him deeper into his seat—and alarming: Marigold's bitten fingers fly to her mouth. "Ignore him, Declan," their mother orders, but in a dull voice Declan answers, "I'm not watching it anyway."

He walks from the room, a barefoot boy who looks small when

he passes his father. Joe's gaze follows him right to the door. *Why do you want this?* Freya would like to know, but it's an impossible thing for a child to ask her father. Their brother has gone, and that can't be changed. His leaving has knocked the corners off the peril they were in. She glances at Syd, who sags desolately in his chair. Say nothing, do nothing, behave as if you are unharmed and this is normal, this thudding heart, the acidic air, this evening bitterly torn. "Come here, Petey-boy." Joe pats the space between himself and Freya. "I'll tell you a story. I'll tell everybody a story." In a few minutes he will be snoring.

She gets abruptly to her feet, refusing to pretend she can listen.

She goes to his room and is surprised to find him buckling on sandals. "Where are you going?"

He taps the shoe into place and stands up. "Not to bed."

She knows he feels his responsibilities, as she does: they are the eldest. "Don't leave. He'll fall asleep—"

But he shakes his head and she sees it then, the damage their father does, a kind of quicksandy pit her brother can only run from. "I'll come with you," she says.

They go down the side of the house that's not overlooked by the lounge-room window. The evening is mild, a few birds still poke around the naturestrips. The gardens they pass are empty, but curtains are open to catch the last of the light and from some houses comes the sound of television, the closing-credits music of the program the Kileys had been watching. There is no evidence of children living in these houses, no tricycles on the lawns or chalkmarks on the paths—Freya likes this about these streets, how they make her uncommon. It's mild and meek and safe here, any one of the people in the houses would help her if she went to their door. She can go from house to house and sign up swathes of sponsors for a readathon. Yet in their silence and goodness they must hear the sounds that come from the Kiley house on the very worst nights—and they keep their doors closed to that. She wonders how anybody could do it.

They have no money to play the pinball at the milkbar, and it is too late to go to the stormwater drain. A few blocks away is a park, a wedge of leftover land with swings and a see-saw standing in a field of silvering tanbark, and they head for it, but when they arrive they find the park occupied by a man sitting alone on a swing, which seems something no grown man should do. He levels on the children an unnerving stare, and the siblings reverse to the footpath. It leaves them nowhere to go, but a destination has become important: they must be going somewhere, not fleeing something. Kids without money aren't encouraged at the milkbar, but Declan says, "We can watch someone play."

So they turn back and walk in that direction, and after a time Freya asks her brother, "What would you do if Mum had another baby?"

"Nothing." He is wielding a stick as if it's a blind man's cane, the tip pinging along the footpath. "What could I do?"

"Wouldn't you be angry?"

"Why would I be angry?"

She rolls her eyes. "Well, for a start, we haven't got anywhere to put a baby."

"We'd find somewhere. A baby's not big."

"But they grow bigger."

"Not for years," he says; and when the only answer his sister gives is an ominous silence, he asks, "Why? Is Mum having another baby?"

"No. I don't know."

"She doesn't look like it."

"I don't know," she says again.

They round a corner like this, Freya dwelling moodily on something Declan is already forgetting, and almost collide with Avery Price in the company of Colt and Bastian Jenson and their father, Rex. All four are eating ice-creams, the expensive kind coated in chocolate and studded with nuts. "Hail, young Kileys!" Rex raises a saluting hand, and that is in fact what he reminds Freya of, a centurion from a matinee movie. He looks the type who would carry a spear and wear a helmet.

Beyond this, she notices several things immediately: that Avery has an elaborately bandaged knee, and that he seems very at-home in the company of these strangers. The younger boy, who looks like some kind of collectable doll, says, "Hi, Deco!" with a friendliness and familiarity that's both affronting and disorienting. And the older one, Colt, again manages to make her feel peculiar, as if her cheeks have become sandpaper and her limbs slightly stretched, without even saying a word. She wants to stay close to him—abnormally close, sort of *gripping* him—while also wishing to erase herself completely from his mind. "Hi, Mr. Jenson," Declan says, and Mr. Jenson replies, "The name's Rex, remember? Mr. Jenson is my father," and it amazes her to realise Avery and her brother and the new neighbours are already good friends: she feels unbalanced, excluded, wonders why she wasn't told about this, and what it all means. "You haven't got ice-cream," Rex Jenson observes. "Shall we go back and get the Kileys some ice-cream?"

"Sure!" yips Bastian.

"You don't have to," says Declan.

"But we want to, don't we, boys?"

So the Kileys fall in with them, Rex leading the way like a ship's figurehead, Freya dawdling at the rear. The little creature, Bastian, chats at Declan: "Where's Syd? Did he go to school today? Did you go to school today? Did you have fun? What's your favourite thing? My favourite thing is art. What's Syd's favourite thing?" She looks between them to Avery, to the blond back of his head, walking in Rex Jenson's shadow, committed to his ice-cream. Her fingers skim the palings of a fence and she lets herself slow, to see what will happen. What happens makes her blood race: Colt glances back. He waits until she catches up to him. "Hi," he says.

She wants to strike him, push him on the road or into a tree; she wants to wrestle him to the ground and pin him, she's strong enough. "Hello," she says dourly.

His ice-cream hasn't left a smudge on his lips; he carries the stick and wrapper bound together in one hand. "Sorry about my dad," he says.

"Your dad's OK," she replies. "What's wrong with your dad?"

Colt says, "He's so . . ." and doesn't bother to say so what, taking for granted she will understand how a parent appears in the eyes of their child. Perhaps he is not an alien or a robot or a person from the cover of a knitting magazine. "Which ice-cream did you have?" she asks, and when he unfurls his palm to show her the wrapper she says, "Oh, I've seen them on the ads. Was it nice?"

"Pretty nice."

"Maybe the peppermint one would be better?"

"I like caramel. But I like peppermint too."

"Yeah, me too," she says.

Which is followed by a silence that would have been scorching hellfire had the milkbar not been luckily and finally right in front of them. Rex waves Declan and Freya past its door and tells them to choose, from the picture panel on the wall, any ice-cream they want, and when the siblings hesitate to select the most expensive he says, "What about this one, the same as the ones we had?" so they agree that they'll have that one too. And when they come out of the shop, the evening air is beautifully mellow and the boys are waiting like friendly dogs, Colt smiling when he sees she's chosen the same flavour he had. Rex is already talking as he rarely stops: "We were just on our way home to change the bandage on Avery's knee. You Kileys are welcome to come with us, if you're not otherwise occupied. I'm sure Tabby would love to see you again, Freya."

In her normal life Freya would baulk at this, because there's no possible reason Tabby Jenson would love to see her again: but on this night things have become imprecise, as if she's stepped through a door of the castle and found herself in a room where the floor drifts like a raft. The crawling unease that her father brings home has been replaced by a heady sense of possibility. Her mother and brothers and sisters are trapped at home without her, and Freya should feel guilty and she does, but Joe is surely asleep on the couch and her mother and siblings can't see her here, it's pointless to feel bad . . . in truth she doesn't know *what* to feel. She never knows, and can't imagine a time when she will know, and worries that this confusion is destined to get worse and worse, and often she wishes there were someone reliable who could take over her living for her.

The Jenson house is one she's passed countless times but hardly noticed; she can't think why, because it suddenly seems an interesting house, built of burnt-red bricks with a garden full of plants she's never seen before. Inside, the walls are a modish beige, not the lilacs and roses of her own house. There's a television in the front room, a hulking thing standing on four shapely wooden legs, but it isn't switched on: Tabby Jenson is reading a book on a bottle-green corduroy couch. It occurs to Freya that she's never seen her own mother reading, not a novel or a cookbook, not even a magazine. Tabby sits up at the sight of her, says, "Oh, hello again, Freya." And as Declan and his friends move off on the lazy tide which seems to carry boys through life, Freya finds herself standing alone in the glassed double doorway, presented to this woman like a gift she hasn't asked for, on the evening of a weekday when — according to Elizabeth Kiley's rules of polite behaviour for children which include no phonecalls after dinner and no following one's host around like a sheep and no answering questions in monosyllables and never, ever, ever entering a parent's bedroom — no unrelated adult should have to endure the presence of somebody else's child. Standing before Tabby Jenson she realises that everything is wrong. She should be at home with her family. "I'm sorry to disturb you," she says.

Tabby smiles. "You couldn't help it. Rex is the Pied Piper."

"I guess," Freya says, although in her recollection the Piper was something like a monster—presumably Mrs. Jenson doesn't mean it that way. She casts about for conversation: there are no toys thrown across the creamy carpet, no records lying like black puddles on the floor, no plates of chewed crusts or upended schoolbags spilling balls of plastic wrap. There's a real flower in the vase on the mantel, and in the corner is a junglish houseplant in a dimpled silver pot. There's a glass-topped coffee table and on it is a thick book about painting. Freya would never have guessed a house in her suburb could be so swish. "Do you like your new home?" she asks.

"Very much, thank you." Tabby's thumb is marking her place in the book. "We'll be happy here."

Freya nods. How drear it must be, she thinks, to be a lady, if conversation must always revolve around whether or not everyone is happy. "What are you reading?"

Tabby glances at the book clamped on her hand, then holds it up for Freya to see. It's a history of a queen who is wearing, on the cover, a white dress positively dirty with jewels. "Are you interested in history?"

"Oh. Not really." Freya is barely conscious of it. From where she stands, with only a dozen years behind her, even the previous month is infinitely past. Her grandparents, uncles, aunts, parents and teachers are about as old as the moon. "I like dinosaurs," she says, and hears herself, and winces. "That's a bit dumb."

"Not at all." Tabby smiles; she looks even prettier, on the corduroy couch, than she had in the church carpark. Her skin is smooth and her dark hair is groomed into waves, and she's wearing lipstick in the house. She doesn't seem much like a mother—it's impossible to imagine her wiping clean a baby's clagged-up bottom. Any sandwiches she would make for her sons' lunches would be healthy, compact and, above all, placed tidily into their lunchboxes. Freya wishes her own mother were more this kind of person, someone in control of her life. "If dinosaurs aren't history," Tabby says, "what is?"

"Yeah," says Freya, and dredges, "My brother Syd is always looking for bones and dead things. He loves stuff like that."

"Boys seem to, don't they?"

"He found a dead rat once, and boiled it in a saucepan to get the fur off. It stank up the whole house."

"How awful." Tabby laughs.

"Mum was mad." Freya bites her lip. There's a large painting above the mantelpiece, it looks like tins of blue paint have been upended on the canvas and swept by a broom. The picture above the mantel in her own house is a landscape of a country lane, which to Freya's mind is preferable, but she can accept that this blue painting is what she should admire more. She wonders what it's like to live in such a house, where everything is new and nothing speaks of what's gone before. She flaps a hand at the hallway down which her brother has disappeared. "I'd better go and find the others."

Tabby Jenson nods; when she smiles, her hazel eyes smile also, which strikes Freya as pleasing. "Don't stay out late. Your mother will wonder where you are. Tell Avery to go home, too. He shouldn't worry his grandmother."

Freya scoffs. "Avery's grandma doesn't worry about him."

"That's what he says. I'm sure it isn't true."

"It is." And because she knows more about Avery Price than anyone in this family could, and because she's eternally indignant over the way he is being raised, she says, "Avery and his sister only live with their grandparents because their mother wasn't feeding them or taking them to the doctor or sending them to school. So Mr. and Mrs. Price have them, but they're old and cranky. It's all right for his sister because she's sixteen, she looks after herself—but she doesn't look after Avery. Nobody looks after him. His clothes never fit him properly, he's always wearing t-shirts when it's freezing cold. They never make his lunches, just give him money for chips. His hair isn't cut, he's never clean, if it rains he gets wet because he doesn't have a raincoat. Nobody ever knows where he is or what he's doing. It's like nobody owns him."

Tabby looks down at the queen on the book's cover. "Poor boy," she says. "It's not easy, raising children. I'm sure his grandparents do the best they can."

"Nope," says Freya adamantly, "no one cares about him."

"I think you do," says Tabby.

It makes Freya clamp her mouth shut and something blocks her throat. She can't remember when Avery first appeared in her life, this boy her brother must have befriended in the usual way but who seems like an animal that lives in the trees and occasionally chooses to descend. There's a possum her father feeds with bread and jam, and Avery is like that: a lawless being which will overcome its instincts for the smallest taste of sweetness. Under his good cheer, he's a desperate thing. "Nobody proper," she says.

Colt sees her step tentatively past the screen door and onto the deck which overlooks the garden; Avery is there, sitting on a bench of the outdoor table, and Colt's father is crouching in front of him. She looks at them and then she looks across the garden, at the trees and the corrugated shed where the bikes and tools are kept, at the arena of churned-up earth and the drifts of bark and leaves that escaped the woodchipper. She gives Colt the excuse to walk away from the pool site, leaving Declan and Bastian to contemplate the wonder that is a hole in the ground.

"It should only be another few days," his father is saying as Colt climbs the deck steps. "They cleared the site—chopped down the necessary trees—and mapped out the space yesterday, and today they used a natty machine to dig away the dirt so the pool will be level. Next come the frame and the walls, then the lining and the filtration system, and finally the water."

"You're so lucky." Freya glances at Colt. "I wish we had a pool."

"You're welcome to come for a swim any time you like. It's for everyone to use."

While he's speaking, Colt's father has been taking from the first-aid box the equipment needed to refresh the bandage on Avery's knee and laying it out in order. He peels away the original strips of sticky plaster saying, "Sorry, sorry," as they tug at Avery's skin, leaving behind tacky shape-shadows of themselves. The wad of padding, stained and off-colour, is glued to the weepy knee: Rex has a basin of water and a sponge, and steadying Avery's calf in his palm he presses the wet sponge onto the padding so water floods down Avery's shin and over the decking and drips through the gaps between the planks into the darkness below, and woozily the pad peels away. Colt watches everything — the press of his father's thumb into the boy's calf, the blink of Avery's grey eyes. Seeing the grotesque injury Freya says, "Avery! That's horrible! How did you do that?" and Avery shrugs and smiles; Rex says, "He's being very brave about it. You're being very brave, Avery."

You bastard, Colt thinks. You *liar.*

His father takes a cloth and wipes the boy's leg until the skin is dry and only the slats of the deck are still splashed. He dabs the cloth about the wound, which is a sickly plasma-yellow but clean, Colt sees, and not infected. "Yes, he's been brave," Rex murmurs, "we're proud of him, aren't we, Colt?" and Colt pretends he hasn't heard. If he cracked open his father he thinks he would find dark, slimy threads running from his father's feet to his brain. From the garden Bastian calls, "Colly? Can we get the BMX out?" and Colt forces it down, says, "It's your bike too, Bas."

"He just likes the attention," Freya says, and Rex chuckles without shifting his focus from Avery. He smooths antiseptic cream into the wound's depths, takes a fresh disc of padding and sets it into place, then reaches for the plaster and scissors. While he binds the knee in a network of strips he mumbles quietly, as if it's an old song, "We all like some attention, don't we? A bit of attention never goes astray." And Colt, watching Declan and Bastian wheel the BMX from the shed, feels the uncoiling of something dragonlike in his chest, something he must bite against to keep from flapping, screaming, into the sky. Then Rex claps his hand to Avery's thigh and gives the boy's leg a shake. "Next time we'll let it air for a while, all right? You can spend a few hours in the playroom letting the air get to it. In the meantime, no bike-riding or fighting or poking around in drains."

"But that leaves nothing," says Freya.

Avery tests the swing of his leg within its plaster scaffold. "Thank you," he says.

"You are free to go, sir." And Avery gets to his feet, but because Rex is gathering the first-aid equipment and the space between the bench and the crouching man is narrow, he bumps Rex's crown with his hip. "Oof," says Rex, and reels dramatically. And Colt actually feels nauseous, his entire body drenched by sickness.

The sky has grizzled over, but it's still scarcely dark; the full moon is as soft and circled as a drop of milk. Avery hobbles across the yard to where Declan and Bastian are tooling around with the bike, and from the deck they watch him go. The earth from the pool excavation has been piled near the fence, and Rex tells Freya, "I thought the boys could use that dirt to build a jump for the bike." And although it's something innocent enough, every nerve in Colt's body tightens impossibly more. He needs, with a feeling close to franticness, for his father to *cease.* He cannot have this in his life, this rangy figure with its helping hands. It's like living with a tiger, something powerful that doesn't care if you die. "Sit," Rex invites Freya. "No formalities in this house."

She chooses a bench that hasn't been splashed with water, and Rex, having packed up the kit, takes the bench opposite her. Colt, leaning against the railing, stays where he is. They watch Declan riding round the garden on the new bike, weaving it expertly between the trees. Bastian is running beside him, laughing in ringing bursts, trying either to catch the bike or to avoid it—Colt doubts that even his brother knows which. "So where were you Kileys headed this evening?" his father asks the girl.

Freya's hands are twined in front of her. "Nowhere. We were just getting away from the house."

Rex tips his head to Bastian and his squealing. "Too noisy?"

"No." She smiles. "It's always noisy at our house. It wasn't because of that." She looks at the table, scratches a fingernail against the wood. "Sometimes, my dad . . ." She pauses, glancing aside, but she wants to say it, Colt sees. She doesn't want to be cowardly or ashamed. "Sometimes he drinks a lot."

He'd have thought his father would make some dismissive reply, but instead Rex says, "Ah. Some men do."

She scratches the table, lifts her shoulders and lets them fall. "I don't know why he does."

"There are probably all sorts of reasons. But none of them would have anything to do with you."

Freya nods, looks over the yard to her brother; she has a pleasant but plain face, as if not much more than the minimum effort has gone into her. She says, "Some nights he tells Declan to get to bed, even when it's not late—when it's hardly even dark. He never says it to Marigold or Dorrie, even though they're little. He only says it to Declan."

Colt, at the railing, watches his father think about this. He has never known Rex to drink too much, so his idea of drunkenness comes from movies in which men stagger along rainy streets singing, beaming goofy smiles. Occasionally cartoon characters guzzle from a keg and slam down on their faces, always wearing that same goofy smile. But Freya's face is darkening, a small snarl against the world.

"Sometimes fathers are jealous of their sons," Rex says, and without question it is the most astonishing thing Colt has ever heard him say.

Freya ponders it, and looks up frowning. "Why would Dad be jealous of Declan?"

Colt's father doesn't reply immediately, his gaze travelling down the steps and into the garden, past the great oval gouge in the earth still marked by the teeth of the digging-machine, across the mulchy garden beds to where the evening shadows are gathering along the fence and beneath the trees. Declan is letting Bastian get close, then shooting the bike out of reach; Bastian trills with amusement as his grasping hands catch air. Avery is holding onto a tree as if anchoring is necessary to stop him joining the game. The plaster strips make it look as though he's put his leg through a remedial web. Just as Colt thinks his father won't answer at all, Rex turns back to the girl. "Maybe," he says, "when your father looks at Declan, he sees someone with his life still ahead of him. Somebody who hasn't made bad decisions, who hasn't failed yet. Somebody like the boy your father used to be. A boy who is gone, and isn't coming back."

Freya frowns and frowns as she thinks about this. "But Declan is his son," she says. "He should be happy about him. Proud of him. Shouldn't he?"

"Yes," says Rex. "But for some men, love is difficult."

The girl gasps as if jabbed; Colt is no less amazed. He has never heard his father speak this way, as if a layer of skin has been shed. "Do you think Dad hates Declan?" she asks, and her eyes are big, her voice hushed. "Does he hate us? Does he think we're . . . a bad decision?"

Rex tips his head. "What do you think he thinks? What does sense tell you?"

She stares and stares. "I don't know. I hope he . . . likes us."

"I'm sure he does." Rex sits back. "I'm sure he loves you. But your father has chosen how he wants to be, Freya. He chose to do what he's done in the past, and every day he is choosing his future. You can't do anything about it except learn from his decisions, so you'll be wiser when it comes to making your own. Perhaps that's one of the unsung gifts a parent gives a child: lessons in what not to do. What do you think, Colt?"

And Colt, who is being dangerously lulled by the sight of this new face of his father's, suddenly remembers what he thinks, and it's all he can do not to snort. The girl, though, gazes at Rex in wonder. For Colt it is laughable, contemptible, enraging; but for Freya, he sees, it is as if she has pulled on a weed and the whole world has come up in her hand.

The filling of the swimming pool attracts them like flies: on Saturday even Garrick is there to watch. The pool has fibreglass walls patterned like timber, and a white, steel-ribbed frame; its gem-blue lining will tint the water a blinding aquamarine. Syd assumed the water would arrive dramatically—trucked in on a lorry and released as a tidalwave—but in fact all that happens is that Rex Jenson drapes the garden hose into the pool and turns on the tap. At first it appears that the filling will happen quickly, for water rushes over the plastic floor and in a few minutes the boys can see their faces reflected in a sparkling pond. Once the hose is submerged, however, time seems to slow within the confines of the pool. The boys spend the morning crafting from the excavated soil a jump for the BMX, and they make regular inspections of the pool, but the water rises slothfully, and sometimes seems to have ceased rising at all. Garrick announces, "We need more hoses. Avery, go and get your hose. Not the one in your pants, that's just a water pistol. You too, Syd—go home and get a hose. Otherwise we're gonna be here all week."

Avery says, "But there's only one tap."

"There are taps in the kitchen," Bastian says helpfully. "There's taps in the laundry."

"Don't worry about it," says Declan. "We'll just have to wait."

Garrick, who's standing with his head hanging over the rim of the pool, gives the fibreglass wall a boot. He digs his teeth into the frame, snuffles doggishly. Syd sees Colt watching him from the far side of the pool. It's another sunny day, and sunshine is reflecting off the lining and painting Colt's face blue. Colt will glide through the water like an eel, Syd thinks; Garrick will bob like a turd. He will delight in pissing in the pool — Syd predicts it with stomach-clenching dread. "This is boring," declares the turd. "Let's get out of here. Let's go down to the drain." He jabs his chin at Colt. "Wanna come?"

Colt pushes away from the pool. "Sure."

"Not me!" chimes Bastian. "I don't want to go!"

"You can stay," says his brother. "Avery can take your bike."

"Bags the BMX," says Garrick.

They hoist the bikes — the BMX and the Jensons' racers, the dinged mongrels belonging to the Kileys — out of the grass and skim down the driveway, Garrick's legs pumping to take him into the lead, streaming past the house toward the road. The air is balmy, it's a perfect day for riding, the kind of soft windless day that can be ridden through forever. As they're bumping over the gutter the screen door bangs and Colt's father calls, "Hey! Where are you going?"

Colt loops a circle on the road, foot scraping the tarmac. "To the drain. Bastian's staying here."

Syd and Declan and Avery loop back, the wheels wheezing through the grip of their brakes; only Garrick speeds away down the hill. Colt's father comes out of the house to the end of the porch, dodging to see past the leafy trees. He is carrying the newspaper he must have been reading. "Is Avery with you?"

The Kiley boys turn to Avery, who looks alarmed but scuds the green racer nearer Colt. He dips his head to find the man beyond the branches. "I'm here, Mr. Jenson."

There's a brief silence. Syd can't properly see Colt's father—from where he's standing, in the centre of the road with his fingers tight to the brake, Avery appears to be talking to the trees, to some malign presence that haunts trees. Then the man says, "What did I tell you about that drain, Avery?"

The tone is familiar to any child, as weighty and as repellent as a wet school jumper. It makes Declan and Syd bridle, and Avery sink his teeth in his lip. "Ah," he says. "It's got germs."

"And why is that fact particularly concerning for you?"

"Um. Because of my knee."

"And what have I told you about riding a bike?"

"Not to do it," says Avery, crushed, "until my knee is better."

The boys stand stiffly on the road, their bikes tilted against their thighs. Syd's cheeks are hot, and he looks away to where Garrick is waiting for them at the bottom of the hill. The boy's hands are on his hips, and Syd can feel his intolerance; any moment will come the blasted shout. From the man among the trees there's a ponderous steamroller of silence: the boys squint into it, hardly able to breathe. Then Avery says, "Well. I won't go."

"Dad," says Colt. "He wants to come with us."

"He's free to do whatever he chooses," Colt's father answers, but the boys hear the impossibility of freedom, the options Avery does not have. "I'm not stopping him. I'm just reminding him to be careful. It'll be a shame to have looked after his knee so well, only to see that effort go to waste."

"It's all right." Avery, squeezing and releasing the racer's brake, looks lamely at Colt. "I'll just go home. It doesn't matter."

"I beg your pardon?" says the man. "What was that? I couldn't quite hear you."

Avery ducks to call past the trees. "I'll go home—"

"No, you don't have to go home. You can wait here with Bastian, if you prefer. There's plenty to do here. But it's entirely up to you, Avery. Go to the drain, if that's what you'd rather. But remember it's you who will live with the consequences."

Syd ogles Declan, who murmurs, "Bloody hell." Colt looks away from his father to the boy beside him. "Come with us," he says, so quietly, his voice dust on the breeze.

"What are you cocks doing?" Garrick screams from the bottom of the hill.

Avery winces. "I better not . . ."

"Hurry up!" Garrick roars.

"I'll just hang around, it'll be OK . . ."

"No, come," says Colt.

And then, because they know what it's like, the unclimbable walls that can rocket up to close a child in, Declan takes pity and says, "Just stay here, Avery. We won't be long. Come on, Syd."

Deftly he spins his pedal into place beneath his toes, and turns his wheel downhill. Colt lingers before following as if there is something else he'd say but, unable to remember, has to let it go; and by the time they reach the pit of the hill he is leading on the red racer, flying like he's glad to be gone.

The stormwater drain is a massive concrete pipe wide enough for a tall boy to walk through without having to stoop. At its base runs a thin greenish thread of never-drying slime, but high on its walls are brown stains testifying to where water has gushed through the drain shoulder-high to torrent out into the creek which trips past the pipe's outlet. On all sides of this creek there is wasteland, a long verdant tail-end of ground that cannot be built on because of the waterway. It's an unlovely, ramshackle place, thrumming with insects, thorny with blackberry and thistle. Rubbish collects here as if called, the trees that slope over the water decorated with debris swept into their branches when the creek rises biblically during storms. Syd, when he comes here, keeps an eye out for a body lodged amid the rocks and scrub. It is his greatest goal, the discovery of a corpse.

The drain is well suited to this gone-to-seed landscape, the way a headstone matches the graveyard that surrounds it. Most of the pipe is buried, only its wide mouth gulping at the air; a few footsteps down its throat carry an explorer away from the heat and light of the sun, into a darkness so dense and cool it's like being inside the body of a gigantic leech. On the pipe's cresting walls are daubs of graffiti, that dong-nosed simpleton Kilroy, a cracked heart dripping a vampiric tear. Once, long ago, Avery had tried to convince Syd that this heart was the secret sign of a gang which used the drain as a hideout, murderers who were watching Syd even as he blinked into the gloom. He tries the line out on Colt, who says, "Oh yeah?" with such complete disbelief that Syd feels foolish all over again. "Nah," he says, "only joking."

Colt walks into the pipe until the light just mists around the ankles of his jeans. He looks up at the curving ceiling, down at the slimy trickle between his feet. "How far have you been through here?" he asks, and his voice rings as voices do in this concrete underworld, as if they are boys made of hammered metal.

"Miles," says Garrick.

"Not far," says Declan. "We need a better torch."

"It's dangerous." Syd slaps the pipe's flank. "You never know when a flood will come gushing down. You'll drown and get torn to pieces if you're in the pipe when it floods."

Garrick says, "It only floods when there's been lots of rain. It's not raining today, is it."

"But sometimes it floods when it's not raining." Even as he speaks Syd wonders where he's sourced this information, and if there's any truth to it, and if he's not in fact making it up. "Water comes from — other places —"

"From where? Your weeny wang? It's a stormwater drain. A *stormwater* drain, got it?"

Syd subsides resentfully, eyeing Garrick through the muzzy light. The bigger boy is lounging in a square of sunshine, back bowed to fit the pipe's curve. If Syd ever finds a dead body, he wants it to be Garrick's. He wants it to be Garrick's, and he wants it to be cold. "I don't see you going into the drain," he says. "Not even when there hasn't been a *storm.*"

"Shut up. You don't know what I do."

"I know you don't go miles down the drain."

"Do you want to?" asks Colt. "We could."

"Oh yeah!" Syd pivots to his brother. "Can we?"

Declan's nose crinkles. "I wouldn't go without a torch. Who knows what's down there."

Colt hears this, and nods shortly, but Syd can tell he's only listening to the advice, not necessarily accepting it, not necessarily making it a rule which applies to him. He isn't afraid, Syd sees, the way Garrick is afraid, and Declan is afraid, and Syd himself is afraid. He stares at a boy he in no way resembles, and although loyal to the bone to Declan, he knows he has found the boy he'd like to be. He would willingly do anything Colt Jenson told him to do—fight Garrick, jump off a roof, sleep overnight in the drain. Garrick, too, is staring at Colt, his feet planted to take the burden of his bending body. "How come your dad's always carrying on about Avery?" he asks.

Colt turns, and particles of sun brush his face, and the blackness of the tunnel hulks behind him. For a moment he doesn't answer, and Syd has the odd idea that he's about to backflip spectacularly away into the darkness. But when he speaks, he's as ordinary as they are. "Dad's a dentist. That's kind of a doctor. He worries about germs."

Garrick sniffs. "Germs should be worried about Avery."

Syd says, "Avery will go into the drain with you, Colt. He's not a scaredy-cat."

Garrick's snake eyes dart to him. "No one's scared. We just need a decent torch."

But Colt is stepping out of the stygian gullet of the pipe, passing Garrick and Syd and Declan, into the fullness of the light. He stands with his toes on the brim of the pipe, looking at the tawny creek and its slouched earth walls, looking into the shabby trees that line the creek's bed. His hands are in his jean pockets, his naked elbows bent. "It's good here," he says.

"Did you have a stormwater drain where you used to live?"

"No. That wasn't a place like this."

"Were you rich before, and now you're poor?" Syd asks. "Is that why you came here?"

"They're still rich, cocko," says Garrick. "Look at all the stuff they have."

"I don't know why we came here," says Colt. "I don't know what difference it will make."

He says it in a thoughtful voice, and the boys glance at each other: it is clear that Colt Jenson is of a breed other than theirs, which isn't necessarily a good thing. "Have you joined an athletics club yet?" Declan asks.

"No. I'm not going to."

"Why not? You shouldn't give up."

Colt shrugs. "It's only running."

"But you've won all those trophies. You must be good at it."

"I reckon I'd be faster than you," says Garrick.

Syd guffaws. "As if!"

"I could be — if we ran here, along the creek. I know the — the terrain."

"The terrain!" Syd's bray of laughter bounces down the pipe. In his mind he sees it, Colt sprinting away like a cheetah, Garrick lurching like a cork.

"He's had more training than me," Garrick concedes, "so I'd have to get a head start. That's fair. But apart from that: be close."

Syd springs off the wall. "OK, let's race!"

"Are you mental?" Declan asks Garrick.

"Why wouldn't I win?" demands the big boy stubbornly. "You haven't seen me run. I'm fast."

Without turning to look at them, Colt says, "I'd beat you."

"Maybe," says Garrick. "Maybe not."

"Let's do it!" Syd dances about. "A long race, or a sprint? Cross-country, or on the path?"

Garrick says, "I didn't say I wanted to race, I was just saying what would happen if we did."

"Ah! Gutless! I knew it!"

"I'm not gutless. I just don't want to embarrass him."

"Embarrass him!" Syd shrieks. "You'd eat his dust!"

"Shut your face." Garrick pushes off from the wall.

"Chicken!" Syd crows, brave to the last. "Bawk, bawk, bawk!"

But it's certainly true he'd never have guessed that someone as bulky as Garrick could move as fast as he does: he lunges across the pipe like a python, smacking his palm into Syd's forehead so the boy's skull ricochets off the concrete with a thunking, searingly painful sound. Declan, Colt and Garrick watch impassively as Syd, clutching his head and sucking his agony in, slides without struggle into the slime at their feet. "Serves you right," says Declan.

On Sunday, Freya decides to go to church after all. She still doesn't believe in God—she's attending for devilish reasons. *The heart is wicked:* it makes her laugh, and Marigold looks at her. Freya is finding that sometimes, when she opens a door of the castle, she's confronted by a startling but not disagreeable new version of herself.

From her place at the end of the pew she can see the family: Tabby in a slim dress the colour of a lime leaf, a pink cardigan slipped over her shoulders, Bastian looking drugged and warbling through the songs druggedly. When Colt bows his head it's tempting to plunge her hands into his hair and see them vanish to the wrist, to shake him in her teeth until he rattles. It genuinely shocks her, the things she imagines these days. Some cackling goblin seems to have taken over her brain. When she's sufficiently composed to look again, her sights glide past Colt to his father. Rex's hair has been brushed back tidily, an iron has left a crease down his sleeve. At one point he reaches over and wipes a curl from Bastian's face, and Freya catches her breath. She can't believe that Rex believes in God. Someone who sees the world through such clear eyes would know that God is a fairy story. She stares across the church at him, willing him to glance at her, anticipating the scramble of her heart if he does; but he doesn't.

When the service ends she'd like to cleave to them, but there are too many people around; she wants a planet where only she and they exist. Miffed, she stalks home alone, sulky not with the Jensons but at the entire intrusive mass of humankind. Maybe, she tells herself, it was for the best. Maybe she would have been stupid, and come away hating herself. Probably: and yet, she craves them. She could have been given the chance.

At home she wriggles under her bed, which is the only place inside the house where she can get some privacy, the bed's valance enclosing the caskety space between floor and mattress pleasingly. Lying with her temple pressed to the carpet, she hears Dorrie come into the room whoo-hooing the music of *Doctor Who*. The little girl rummages in her schoolbag and finds what she's searching for, and skitters off like something twanged from a catapult yelling, "Mum!" Minutes later she hears her father's footsteps coming down the hall, the unlocking of the side door to let the afternoon air circulate. Joe likes fresh air, open windows, his children to be outdoors. Freya considers what he would say if she stuck her head past the valance and told him, "I'm hiding under the bed." He wouldn't ask why, was she troubled, was she sad? He would say, "It's a nice day, go out and play."

After lunch he is working on Elizabeth's station wagon: there's often something wrong with the car, it leaks oil, it sweats fluid, its motor makes a dire regurgitating sound. Its bonnet is forever yawning open on the prop of a metal stick. Drifting up on bare feet, Freya tells her father, "This car is a bomb." Joe, bent over the engine, doesn't look up; he says, "Well, it shouldn't be." It shouldn't be, but it is.

She likes to watch him working on cars, she's learned a great deal by doing so. Carburettor, alternator, radiator, plugs; if the engine won't catch make sure that the radio and headlights are off; you can't push-start an automatic. She likes it when he needs her to turn over the ignition while he listens to the motor. "Give it some juice," he'll tell her, which means she must press the accelerator, and it's unfailingly thrilling, the beastly roar that is the vehicle's response to her touch. Her father has a cloth that he uses to wipe his fingers but the grease never completely cleans away and she admires how this doesn't trouble him, it seems the right way a man should be. "Shoo, shoo." He waves her aside, and she retreats to the shade slanting off the side fence to await his next command. She thinks about asking him if there will be a new baby, but the question simply won't assemble itself in her mouth. Instead her mind wanders to something bizarre: how her father, leaning over the vehicle, is like a dentist. A car dentist, poking around clunky teeth.

Declan glides up the driveway on his bike, casting only a glance at his father and sister. The workings of automobiles do not interest him. "Where have you been?" asks Freya.

"Colt's."

The word is a zap. "Where's Syd?"

"He's there too."

Declan dumps his bike on the path and goes into the house

and comes out a minute or two later, and deigns to stop by the station wagon on his way across the yard. "There's a barbeque at the Jensons' tonight," he tells them. "Everyone's invited—you too, Dad. Mum says we can go."

Their father doesn't lift his head. "Who are the Jensons?"

It's incredible to Freya that anyone could be unaware of these people who are so effortlessly taking up so much space in her life. Excitement romps through her, she wants to jump and squeal: then she remembers sitting on the deck and telling Rex that her father drinks too much. The secret had spilled out of her like some low-slung thing, and she hadn't expected the relief it would be, to speak it out loud. But standing beside her father, seeing the grease on his hard-working hands, she feels her disloyalty. She loves him, but she's harmed him. The heart is wicked. "New neighbours," she says, "up the road."

He says, "Hmm," and straightens, staring into the engine with his thumbs either side of the fierce hook which keeps the bonnet down. His son and daughter gaze at him. In some way or another they are always gazing at him, always struggling to be one step ahead of what is coming. Joe is not a sociable man, and he keeps his world small. His workmates at the printing plant and a few friends he's known since childhood are enough for him. So when he says he will come to the Jensons' barbeque, it is completely surprising, and Freya can't work out why he has agreed. Maybe, she thinks later, it is to ensure the new neighbours won't think of him as the bad man of the neighbourhood.

They've been told to bring nothing except an appetite but Elizabeth makes a potato salad, and they walk up the road as a family for the first time in Freya's memory, Dorrie swinging her mother's hand, Joe wheeling Peter in his stroller, and Syd trotting ahead and returning like a hound. It's dusk, not yet night-time, because the Jensons know the Kileys have young children and also that it is a school night. Freya's both hopeful and worried that they will be the only guests, so she's disappointed and relieved to see strangers on the deck, the neighbours who live either side of the Jensons and a shy-looking woman from over the road. Rex is discussing wine with this shy lady when they arrive, so Freya stumps down into the garden to where the children are, to where Colt is: and the strange and witchy thought comes to her that she hopes Rex regrets it, watching her go.

Though they've lived in the brick house for just the shortest time, already it is a boys' backyard: a bike track serpentines between the trees, around the pool and over the earth jump, and the garden beds are scattered with crashed Matchbox cars. Freya's sisters, however, swoop down on it like seagulls, and easily seize control. The BMX is wrested from Bastian by Marigold, and Avery limps alongside her as she ploughs round the earthy course while Garrick says, "OK, that's enough, you've had enough, it's not a bike for girls," each time they sail past him. It's a cool night for swimming but Syd jumps into the pool, his chest snowy-white and his arms sleeved with sunburn, pencil legs sticking out the mouths of too-big shorts. At the end of the yard, where the scrub is thick, Colt and Declan are messing about with the bike jump, packing dirt into the hillock; they're talking together in a private way which makes Freya demand, "What? What?"

Declan says, "Nothing. I was just wondering why Garrick's here."

Freya likes Garrick as much as anyone does; he has no charms to offer a girl. She looks across the yard to where he's saying to Marigold, "It's a boys' bike — see that bar? That's called a *dick bar.* Girls don't have dicks. That's what makes it a boys' bike." And Declan, she realises, is correct: a family barbeque is not the place she'd expect to find the neighbourhood lout, and his presence is suddenly offensive beyond telling, a stone in a bowl of cream. "Why did you invite him?" she asks Colt.

"I didn't." Colt smiles. "He invited himself. He wanted to come. He was the first to arrive." He turns to the jump, stamps a foot on its rump. "He brought a packet of biscuits."

The sheer gall of it is outraging; she glares through the trees as Marigold jounces past and Garrick says, "You're gonna hurt yourself and start crying, you know!" Beyond them she can see, on the deck, Rex offering his guests a platter of flesh-coloured morsels pierced by toothpicks. Bound by politeness, he would have accepted Garrick Greene's biscuits with the same grace as he'd greeted Elizabeth's salad, for which Freya had peeled a dozen potatoes. To Colt she says, "You don't like him though, do you? I don't. I hate him. I really hate him."

And Colt, to her horror, replies, "I don't hate him," as if Garrick and Freya are scarcely different in his eyes, the way shop-bought biscuits are just as good as homemade salad: if anything, Freya feels herself judged the lesser of the two. She looks to Declan to back her up but instead of denouncing Garrick as a pest and a fool he says, "He's OK, don't worry about it." And she feels suddenly drained, heart-broken: surrounded by misunderstanding, she turns and walks away.

Syd is swimming along the bottom of the pool, worm-sleek, arms scything, his hair a silver cap smoothed perfectly to fit his skull. His legs seem lengthened, and hinged like a cricket's. Freya stops, pretending to watch him. Behind her eyes are tears like prickles. No one thinks about her, takes notice of her, or cares if they've hurt her feelings. Everyone has a friend or something to do, but she has nothing and no one. She wishes she were home, curled up reading in her bedroom, and considers saying she feels sick and leaving, but that's not the solution she wants. She keeps her sights fixed on the glinting water until the tears have seeped away; then she squares her shoulders and heads for the deck, to where the adults are. She can only be the person she is: brave, honest, clear-eyed. Not a child. Passing Marigold on the BMX she snaps, "You've had enough now, give someone else a go." And is infuriated, looking around, to see that Garrick has in fact lost interest in claiming the bike, and is over at the jump instructing Colt how to pile the earth higher.

On the deck her mother is talking to the people who live beside the Jensons, and her father is standing on the outskirts, by the rail, a glass in his hand and his sights rested on nothing. "Hello, Freya," says Tabby Jenson, and Freya says, "Hello." There's something about the woman, Freya then and there decides, that she doesn't like. Her mind is moving freely now, slashing and burning as it goes. Bastian Jenson has climbed the pool's ladder and is screeching for Syd to come up for air. The boy is more like a rodent than a child, the kind of nervous pet whose company wears thin after a few ammonia-tinged weeks. Cruel Colt, fake Tabby, mad Bastian: she feels sorry for Rex.

"Freya," he says, startling her. She hadn't seen him come close. "Are you all right?"

He's wearing an apron which says KISS THE COOK—it looks ridiculous, but he doesn't care. "I'm OK," she says, and magically is: grumpy Freya is stuffed aside and the cheerful version jack-in-the-boxes out. "Are you sure?" Rex asks, looking closely at her. "You seemed a bit upset. Were those boys giving you a hard time?"

Her chin wibbles, she's so touched. "I'm OK," she says again, and she doesn't want to remember being any other way. He flashes his white smile, lets the subject go. "Come on," he says, "come and get something to eat."

And it's lovely to step across the deck with him, lovely to be the subject of his concern as he prods the barbeque meat with tongs, presenting its best face to her. Smoke rises from the grill, dots of fat ping and fly. From the steaks and sausages and onion rings as well as things she's never seen cooked on a barbeque—corn cobs, chicken wings, slices of eggplant and capsicum—she chooses one of the flat burgers that her family has contributed to the feast, the kind which comes in an icy box from the supermarket freezer. Rex says, "That one? That's all? Some eggplant—no? All right, that one's got your name on it." It needs a few more moments on the heat and he moves it aside with the tongs, it now being too special to mingle. He fills a glass with ginger-beer, passes it to her and says, "Cheers!" She smiles and lingers, sipping her drink, entranced by his nearness, which is like that of a strong animal that's had its teeth and claws removed. Smoke and the scent of burnt honey come from the cooking, and now and then flames jump through the grill to lick the meat. There's a tape recorder by the back door, and the music is just loud enough to keep a conversation private. Because she will not behave like a child around him, she asks, "Did you meet my dad?"

"Joe? I did. He's a printer, is that right?"

She watches her father from the corner of her eye. "He's the foreman. He used to work the machines, but not anymore, now he's the foreman. But he's still a printer."

"Then he's just the man I'm after." Rex shovels up a steak and flips it; bands of char mark it like surgical scars. "I want some brochures printed for the surgery. *Have your teeth fixed by the fantastic Doctor Rex!* With pictures of people looking either delighted or terrified, I can't decide. Your dad's got just the expertise I need."

She looks at her father, standing alone by the rail with a fresh glass of beer. She's never thought of him as a man with expertise. He is watching Syd swim; when his son bobs up he calls, "Use your legs to push off from the wall, Syd!" but Syd doesn't hear or simply refuses to, which makes Joe shake his head and tell nobody, because nobody is talking to him, "He'd go much faster if he used his legs." And Freya feels the ache which always lives below the surface no matter what else she feels for him, and must look away: and finds that Rex, too, has paused, the greasy tongs closed on air. "He seems like a decent man, Freya," he says. "I'm sure it's what he wants to be. Your hamburger's ready, if you'd care to bring a plate."

And suddenly the deck is swarming with children who have sensed the imminent arrival of food: a space is cleared on the table between the salads and the bread-sticks, and a platter of meat is placed down; the plates and cutlery and serviettes and food disappear in pieces so the table is like the tasty body of something and the children and adults are carnivorous birds, pecking until only scraps remain. The older boys eat on the deck steps, Avery with his injured leg stretched out, Syd with a towel around his shoulders and his hair slick on his forehead. Bastian dips a hamburger in sauce and nibbles its crispy hem; when he's finished he snuggles into his mother's side, his arms linked about her waist. Tabby folds an arm around him, and it occurs to Freya that her own mother never does such cosy things, and that maybe Tabby is better at being a mother than she looks, and that her own mother is worse. Marigold and Dorrie sit side-by-side on the deck's edge, their bare feet dangling into space, messy plates on their knees. The adults sit around the table on matching canvas chairs, Joe working through a modest meal using a knife and fork and never his fingers, her mother shielding her mouth with a hand while she chews. Rex reclines, hands clasped behind his head, his long legs crossed at the knees. His apron is slung over the barbeque's handle, as if kissing-time is done. After a few minutes he is back on his feet, filling glasses, fetching ice, flipping the music tape. "How was that burger?" he asks as he passes, and she blushes because although it was delicious she now sees that it was shameful, preferring a dubious disc of offcuts to the proper food that was on offer. Even Bastian had chosen one of the hamburgers made by his mother, in which bits of parsley and diced onion could be seen.

Her father is a man of silences. He never talks about himself or anyone else. He mustn't, Freya's long ago reasoned, be interested, not even in himself. So it's surprising when he asks, out of the blue, "What made you become a dentist, Rex?"

Rex, at the barbeque, turns at the waist to look at him. "I wanted to frighten small children." He winks at Freya, which makes her grin, but Joe taps a finger on his plate and says, "It's probably not something you just wake up one day and decide."

Rex wags his head and agrees, "No, it wasn't like that. But I don't suppose it was much different from you becoming a printer. Life takes you places."

"People don't ask me why I became a printer." Joe gives his plate a small shove, and leans back in his seat. "Whereas I guess you get asked about being a dentist pretty often, wouldn't you. It's that kind of job. Not one you just fall into."

"Dad," says Freya, because there's an impoliteness in his tone that surely she's not alone in hearing, and they are guests here, and he is her father around whom it's impossible to be free of the fear that something is about to go wrong. "Maybe he doesn't want to talk about it."

Rex, though, is unruffled. He's been scooping the dregs of the barbeque onto the platter and now he comes to the table and sets the platter in its place, and slips into his seat. "Have you ever had a bad tooth, Joe?" he asks.

He's not a complainer, he's tough as a boot, but he says, "Of course."

"It was all you could think about, wasn't it?" Rex gives a quick dash of a smile. "It was the master of your world. Every moment of the day and night you were at the mercy of this pounding tyrant in your head. You couldn't sleep. You couldn't eat. Nothing was amusing or engaging. You found yourself thinking that if you have to live with this tooth much longer, you'd prefer to die. Your body seems to hate you, after all. It seems intent on driving you to your grave, and you start to think you're happy to go."

Joe says, "Well, it wasn't that bad."

Rex smiles again, reaching for some bread. Everyone, Freya sees, has stopped to listen, even the boys on the steps—although not Colt, he is the exception, he is peering at his feet smoothing dust from between his toes and paying no apparent attention at all. He must have heard it before, this incantation of misery. "It was almost that bad, though, wasn't it?" Rex says. "I bet that tooth ruled your life for a while there. And do you remember, when you had that bad tooth, the one person you wanted to see more than anyone else in the world?"

"The dentist!" chirps Marigold.

"The dentist." Rex nods and sits back, pulling the crust from the bread. "I knew from my very first toothache that it was what I wanted to do. I wanted to be the man who could ease suffering when suffering was a person's whole world."

"You wanted to help," says Tabby.

"You wanted to be a hero," says Joe.

"Joe!" says Elizabeth.

But Joe is scornful. "You wanted—what, a bit of power over people when they're weak?"

"Dad!" Freya's face flames so red it must glow: she'd slap her father, stab him, pick up the platter and swing it at his head. But Rex says, in a hearty voice, "My goodness, I've never thought of it like that! Here I was thinking I just wanted to be of some use! I never realised it was all about power."

He gazes around the deck, smiling broadly, like a lighthouse, and everyone at the table—the next-door neighbours, the shy lady, Elizabeth, Tabby, Freya more than anyone, Freya as if her life depends on it—smiles back as forcefully as they can. "Maybe

I'd better throw in the towel!" Rex laughs. "From now on, my patients can just put up with their pain. Some of them certainly deserve it. What do you reckon, Bas?"

Bastian jerks to life. "Yeah!"

"A hero. A hero. Goodness me. I've never thought of that." Rex, chuckling, drops the mutilated bread onto his plate and smears his fingers on a tattered serviette. "Although one thing I do know, and I'll tell you this, Joe: if I was a hero, I'd charge a lot less money. Or maybe a lot more? One or the other."

His guests laugh and laugh enthusiastically. Freya laughs too, though nothing is funny. Colt, she sees, hasn't looked up from his feet, but he has gone still. He must have been listening after all—listening to Freya's father prove himself as mean as she told them he was. It should make her feel better, but she's washed with dismay. "Is it too soon for dessert?" asks Tabby as the amusement fades. "We don't want to keep you forever, shall I serve dessert?"

There's a rush of chair-shunting, plate-stacking, table-clearing, door-swinging. Desserts are brought out, fruit salad and cake and ice-cream and pavlova, and the younger children jostle jealously at the table for their share. "You must have been cooking all day!" marvels Elizabeth, and Tabby says, "Oh, I bought the pavlova, I only did the cream and passionfruit." Marigold shivers and says, "I hate passionfruit," and Freya could thump her, her whole family is monstrous, she can scarcely swallow the cake. She begs for the night to be over, and her life with it. The boys eat hurriedly and then move back into the garden, Garrick grabbing the BMX but not before he has taken a cleansing plunge in the pool, bombing off the top rung of the ladder, splashing Bastian when the boy comes within reach. The plaster on Avery's knee is black, petalling at the edges; he and Declan and Colt ride the skateboards down the driveway. Syd, who waited for Garrick to vacate before slithering into the water, claws his way around the bottom of the pool like an otter exploring a river. Joe stands at the rail watching him, and when Rex comes to stand beside him the men glance sideways at each other, and Freya feels sick with trepidation. But all Rex says is, "What do you know about building, Joe? I'm hoping to extend the deck around the pool," and although Freya has never known her father to build anything, never even seen him swing a hammer, he answers as if he knows exactly what he's talking about. And Rex, instead of being angry, laughs and nods and asks questions, and changes his plan to encompass Joe's idea: and Freya is completely confused all over again about the way the world works.

As soon as the cake and ice-cream are finished, Peter finds reason for grizzling: Elizabeth says, "We should go." All the adults decide to leave at once then, though it's hardly late: everybody stands up as if there's a race to get out the door. Salad bowls and sandwich trays are rinsed and returned, and Tabby gives Dorrie a little purse of clingwrap containing the sugar flowers from the cake. "You coming?" Avery asks Garrick, who is still haring about on the BMX. "I don't have to leave just 'cause you are," he answers, but Declan says, "Yeah you do, everyone's going home." Garrick says, "Bloody hell!" and throws down the bike. Freya looks at Colt, who quirks an eyebrow, and she finds with surprise that she's not cross or fearful or hurt, just as Rex had not been — that, in fact, her heart is fizzing. And she cannot understand what is happening, why the world keeps changing every time she thinks she has a grip.

They're drifting down the driveway with Bastian trotting round like a chatty satellite when they notice someone is missing: Syd hasn't come out of the pool. "I'll get him," says Declan, and Colt and Freya follow him back up the driveway to the side gate. "Come on, Syd!" Declan calls, but their brother answers with only a rude splash. "Go and get him," Freya tells Declan, but Rex, who's appeared behind them, says, "I'll do it, you two get going." He saunters across the yard, clapping his hands for the boy's attention, crying, "All water babies out!"

Syd's head pops up, streaming, gummy-eyed; the water is cold, and as he climbs down the ladder in the glare of the outside lights he looks bleached to the bone. His towel is on the path, wet and bundled like a drowned cat, but Rex holds out a dry one, something plush which must belong to the family. He drapes it around Syd's shoulders and with his big hands dries the boy's arms and chest and legs, not slipshoddedly, as Syd might dry himself, but thoroughly and with order, as if it's a job to do properly or not at all. He wipes Syd's tummy, his ears, the drips that run down his face. Syd, feather-light, is knocked this way and that, but he doesn't resist, so it's all done in moments; then the boy grabs his clothes and runs to his siblings, wearing only his bathers. "Wait for me," he says, as if they weren't already. Declan says, "Get going," and shoves him in the direction of the street. Freya, as she goes, waves a hand at Colt. "Bye," she says. And he looks at her swiftly, but says nothing.

Their father has drunk just enough to do what, for the children, is the most exciting thing any human being could possibly do: he rummages in the garage for the tin of petrol, and as Elizabeth retreats into the house saying, "You're crazy, you'll kill yourself," he clears back his audience, swigs a mouthful of petrol, and, as the children watch in bitten-lip awe, holds a lit match to his face and blows out a streak of flame. Spectacular, impossible, their own private circus: the children cheer like savages. Marigold screams, "Do it again, Dad, do it again!" and he does, brightening the fair heads of his offspring with dragon-fire. He takes another mouthful and blasts at the sky a spear of orange fire, and they hear its ragged breath, feel its brawny punch, catch its brilliance in their eyes. "Again, again!" shouts Dorrie, but Joe gags, "Oh no, that's enough," and staggers indoors, half-poisoned, spitting as he goes. The sky is dark, and the air is much cooler, but Freya lingers in the yard after Avery and Garrick are gone and her siblings are all inside, remembering how this day started, and the points at which it pivoted from ordinary to appalling to unforgettable.

Colt helps his mother bring the last plates in, then folds up the deckchairs and lugs them to their corner of the laundry. The bicycles and skateboards lie strewn about the yard, and he wheels the bikes into the shed and wipes down the skateboards before returning them to the playroom. Never in his life has he left a possession outside to be ruined by the weather. Bastian is more careless, and Colt walks around with a bucket picking small abandoned vehicles out of the mulch. There are scraps of food dropped about, and he throws them deep into the garden. The earth surrounding the pool is muddy from Syd's splashings, and the muck sticks to Colt's bare feet; he washes them clean under the tap. He looks around but there is nothing left to do outside, and the sky is purple now, overcast by night. Through the window he sees his father moving from fridge to drawer to kitchen counter, his face with its shapely jaw and halo of mahogany hair very calm, quite expressionless, as if the drawer and fridge contain nothing, and nothing was what he expected to find. Even when he opens his mouth and makes some reply to Bastian who must be at the table or in the hall, his face is as empty as something never used. He lives within his body, Colt thinks, like a frightened person might live behind a strong wall. But Colt had seen him rattled tonight, and he knows that, inside, his father will still be shaking.

He brushes his teeth at the bathroom sink, staring as he does so at his reflection in the mirror. He looks a great deal like his father. He has the same heavy hair, the same black-lashed eyes. His nose, like his father's, is square at the tip. He snarls at the mirror, sees his father's white teeth. Even the hand around his toothbrush, with its oversized knuckles and flat fingernails, is the same. It is as if he is being dragged remorselessly to a place he'd rather not go. He spits in the sink, turns the tap off tight. There's nothing he can do about how he looks.

Bastian is in bed, proclaiming like a roosting bird his final thoughts of the day. "Mum, will I have a tuckshop order tomorrow?"

His mother answers from her bedroom, something which Colt, drying his face, doesn't properly hear. "Did you write I get a doughnut?" Bastian asks. "A strawberry doughnut? Is it the one with jam? Can you make sure? Last time they gave me the one without the jam."

Again his mother answers, something soothing, and Bastian subsides. Then his voice lilts out: "Colly, where are you?"

Colt sits on his bed, facing the trophy boys. They are always running, running, striving to be somewhere. Most of them have one raised foot which will never touch the ground. "What, Bas."

"Will you help me carry my bag in the morning? It's really, really heavy."

Their faces are blurred and sightless, their mouths sealed with gold. Already he is losing the memory of what his old friends looked like. "Yeah."

"What?"

Colt lifts his voice. "I will."

"Uh. Colly?"

"What?"

"I don't like it when Garrick rides the BMX. He's too rough." Colt slips his t-shirt over his head, reaches under his pillow for his pyjamas. "The BMX will be all right."

"He's going to break it."

"No he isn't."

"If he breaks it, I will kill him. I will stick him with a knife."

"Bastian." Their father speaks from the front room. "Quiet now. School in the morning."

He is not a child who requires two tellings, and goes silent. Colt steps out of his jeans and underwear and into his pyjama trousers. He checks his schoolbag, which is packed and ready, his homework long done. He excels at school, is a clever and diligent boy who has never brought home a bad report card, and never will. He doesn't know what he will do with his life, but he knows what he won't do. He zips the bag, goes to the door and draws it almost shut.

He reads in bed for a while, trying not to think. The television is on in the front room, his father watching alone. Eventually Colt switches off his bedside lamp, and the room goes dark. Shortly after, he hears the television likewise turned off. He hears his father walk down the hall to the bathroom, where he brushes his teeth and uses the toilet and washes his hands as if they're covered in soot; then he tours the house, checking the doors and windows, switching off the last lights. He goes to the bedroom he shares with Tabby, and Colt is surprised to hear the mild voice of his mother. She could have been asleep by now; she could have pretended to be asleep.

She says something, and Rex replies. There are many walls between the bedrooms, and Colt can't clearly make out the words. He hears just the tone, something like the shush of waves. Normally he wouldn't listen, wouldn't want to listen, but tonight something had happened that doesn't usually happen. Joe Kiley had seen something less impressive than what he was supposed to see. Colt sits up on an elbow, and it seems to help: he hears his father say, "I'm not in the mood to discuss this." Tabby answers, and her voice has a pulled thread: Rex replies, and his voice has a spine. Tabby speaks again, and Rex answers sharply, almost endlessly: "I'm puzzled as to why you'd even mention it. Puzzled and disappointed. I'm extremely tired, and I wish to go to sleep. I was under the impression you were on my side, Tabby. Please let me know if that's not the case."

It's a tone Colt has heard his father use before, a kind of arrogant whine, the sound of some frustrated night-hunting animal or an accused prince. It drags Colt back to the old house, the knock on the door which came without warning one evening, the faces in the hallway like concrete masks over faces he knew. The hung heads, the rubbed jaws, the ones who didn't look up from the carpet, the others who stared like snakes. He'd taken Bastian to his room and they'd sat on the bed, and although he couldn't answer Bastian's questions he had known what was happening the way a body knows it is mortally ill. Now, in this new room, he curls up on the bed, drawing the blankets to his shoulders and the pillow over his face; but the sense of a nightmare follows him under, like a song he cannot shake.

For a couple of days Syd becomes obsessed with Christmas, having caught the fever of imminent gift-getting from his sisters. He and Marigold and Dorrie make lists of things they want. Dorrie's requests run to plastic babies and fluffy animals, as well as to shoelaces, which is odd. Marigold wants polka-dot bed linen, which is also odd. When Syd thinks of what he wants, he pictures the Jensons' playroom but writes one word: *skateboard.* "How long until Christmas?" the little girls ask, and Syd unhooks the calendar from the kitchen wall and shows them. Only the flip of a page, yet still it is weeks, box after box of days. Marigold magnets her wishlist to the fridge, but Dorrie, disheartened, throws hers away. A page is a lifetime to her.

His mother tells him he can't make a pest of himself by visiting the Jensons during the week, and while he obeys he does so in suffering. It is possible to feel summer in the breeze, and he longs to go into the water, to sweep the heavy liquid between his fingers and have the arch of his feet knock against the ungiving floor of the pool. The water will be cold but the prospect is inviting, the way pressing a bruise feels nice. He will stay underwater as long as he can, ignoring his body's protest against the chill and the absence of oxygen. He had discovered, at the barbeque, that he likes swimming for the solitude of it: although in no way an antisocial child, he had found tranquillity in that water. He'd been aware of the world beyond the pool's walls, but he had been cushioned from it. In the water there were no words he couldn't spell, no broadbeans he had to eat, no hand-me-downs that were all he had to wear. There'd been no tight-lipped school principal, no shrivelling before the leather strap, no girls in the playground whispering to each other as he walked by. No maths tests returned with a wrathful F inside a circle. No silver balls disappearing, with his pocket money, down the gutter of the pinball machine. No stink-breathed bullies, no interrupted television shows, no sisters disappointed on Christmas morning. No waking already weighted down by what lies between that moment, and when he can sleep again. The only place he knows that might be the pool's equal as sanctuary is the stormwater drain, but that's too far away for a school night, so all he can do is wander, each evening, round the corner and up the hill to the vicinity of the red-brick house in the hope that the Jensons will see him, sense his longing, invite him in. What actually happens is that he sees Mrs Jenson close the lounge-room curtains, and he sees the man briefly through what must be the parents' bedroom window. He sees, in addition, Avery's banged-up bike in the front garden. It is there, on the driveway, on Monday evening, and it is there, by a tree, on Tuesday. Disturbingly, on Tuesday not only is Avery's bike in the garden, but Garrick's is too. There's no evidence that either of them is swimming in Syd's pool, but the thought of Garrick Greene polluting the blue water with his body literally makes Syd feel queasy, and give up.

Late on Wednesday when the children are in bed and it seems the night will pass uneventfully, the car turns into the driveway and the light of headlamps sweeps across the ceiling of the boys' bedroom. Syd hears Declan shift beneath his blankets, and the brothers listen in silence to the slamming of the car door, the unlocking of the house door. Their father's tread is heavy for a lightly-made man. Their mother is in the lounge room, ironing; the boys hear, between their parents, a curt exchange of words. They hear their father move to the kitchen, the dinner plate rattling off the oven's wire shelf.

Syd is aware he isn't breathing, that he had more air underwater than he has now, in his bed, in his room. He listens, and the house has stopped breathing. When the crash comes he knows exactly what it is — the plate hitting the wall. He knows exactly what he will see when he runs to the kitchen — the plate in many pieces, food across the floor. Declan throws aside his blankets and runs for the door. "Stay here," he tells Syd, and disappears. Syd, sitting up, sees Freya rush past, and already the shouting has started, his father's cursing, his mother's rage. After a moment he jumps from bed and charges down the hall pursuing his siblings. He cannot stay behind.

The kitchen is lit fluorescently, too harshly for its size; his father rampages in this cell of whiteness, ignoring the woman and children who crowd the doorway. He has knocked the pile of junkmail from the counter, and the catalogues have slipped under the table and lodged among triangles of shattered plate. Now he's swaying before the refrigerator, one hand gripping its open door, pulling from the shelves one item after another, swearing and weaving as he does so. Onto the floor goes a carton of milk, a bundle of ham, a bowl of leftover bolognaise. Milk glugs from the carton's spout, spaghetti slops from the bowl. The margarine skids thickly across the linoleum. "Dad!" cries Freya. "Stop!" but he doesn't look to them. A jam jar hits a cupboard as loudly as a bomb. On the wall above the table is a smear of mashed potato. The table is splattered with gravy, beaded with peas. Their father wrenches open the crisper, pulls from it a sheaf of carrots and hurls this over a shoulder. The orange spikes and green stems pinwheel under a chair. Any other time, the sight would have made Syd laugh. Now there's a stink in the air, and his heart is racing. His wrist is grasped and he looks up at his mother, and when he looks back to the kitchen his father loses his hold on the fridge door and stumbles sideways onto the floor.

For an instant Elizabeth's hand moves to cover Syd's eyes. "Come away," she tells her children. In the lounge room Declan hurries to the glass doors and opens them, and the evening air billows in. Syd sees stars and, in the street, the glowing orb of a streetlight. From down the hall they hear a plaintive cry and Elizabeth says, "Sydney, go to the girls." He doesn't want to, but already she's steering him to the door by the wrist she still holds painfully. "Hurry," Declan says, and Syd goes. Passing the kitchen he glimpses his father on his knees among the torn papers and strewn food. He runs into his parents' room and Peter is awake in the darkness, climbing from his cot; he lifts the child over the bars cooing, "Baby boy, baby boy," and jostles down the hall with his brother squeezed to his hip. At the furthest room he flicks on the light to find Dorrie and Marigold on Dorrie's bed, bunched up in blankets and nighties. Dorrie is weeping into the hair of a doll, and Marigold, white-faced, has fingers in her mouth. He shovels Peter between them, begging, "Quiet, Dorrie, it's all right, I'm here," but his sister's mouth sags woefully, she buries her face in her doll. "Is it Dad?" asks Marigold. Syd's heart is still racing, hitting at his ribs; when a howl comes from the lounge room, a sound not of pain but of indignation, it whips him round to the door and spills tears down Marigold's face. Peter groans and claws at her, trying to fasten himself to her neck. They hear Freya's strident voice over Elizabeth's angry cries, and Syd heaps the blankets around the children frantically, trying to bundle them into place. "Stay here," he tells Marigold. "Don't come out. Look after Peter and Dorrie." Peter's arms wrap her like pythons, but he meets her blue eyes and she's smart, she understands. Dorrie collapses howling, but Syd doesn't wait.

His father has found his way into the lounge room and stands with his back to the door. There's a dark stain down his trousers which halts Syd like a chain. Joe is weaving as if he's been hit, and perhaps he has been: Elizabeth, in the centre of the room, has the clothes iron gripped in her fist. Declan and Freya flank her like young wolves, Freya shouting at Joe, "What's wrong with you?

Get out, we don't want you! You stink, you're disgusting! Go on, get out! Get out, get out, get out, get out!" And maybe it's the sheer force of her fury that drives him away, because she's small and so swattable, yet their father is going. He's swearing at her, sneering, yet he's going, shifting backwards with his arms up, feeling his way into retreat. Syd sidesteps into the kitchen as his father backs past, harried as he goes by his offspring who dash at him, snarling and yelping, always beyond reach. Hissing with defeat, their father turns and makes for the front door and bangs through the flyscreen. Syd runs to the lounge windows to see him get in his car and haul the door closed—but the engine doesn't start, the headlights don't come on, and for moments the four of them watch breathlessly, Elizabeth still holding the iron. Then she says what the children have realised: "He's fallen asleep. The stupid fool."

Only now, in safety, do they look at each other, and look around the room. Syd sees what made his sister so incandescent: the clothes which their mother spent the afternoon ironing have been torn to the floor and trampled by boots that have left their imprints in gravy. His father's workshirts are among the wreckage, as well as the girls' school dresses. Syd is frightened and wide-awake and still half-dizzy with dread, but it is the sight of all that wasted work which brings hot tears to his eyes.

And then Marigold and Dorrie and Peter have rushed in, weeping wetly, hanging off their mother's arms. Freya kneels and hugs Dorrie. "Don't cry, stop crying," she says. "There's nothing to cry about." But Freya herself looks blanched and ill, and when she lets go of Dorrie her hands are shaking; she gouges her eyes and says, "Oh." For a minute they stand around stupefied, but in truth this is nothing they haven't seen before. Marigold wipes her face, looks at the ravaged ironing and says, "Phew, what a mess!" She and Declan pick up the clothes, hang them on doorknobs and over the backs of chairs. The kitchen needs mopping, broken things must be binned. Syd and Freya clean the floor and walls, but soon Elizabeth sends them to bed.

Lying once more in the dark in his bedroom, the sheets beneath him cool but not cold, Syd marvels how it's possible to think it was a dream. He was in bed before, and he's in the same bed now. He is Syd, as he was before. They will wake in the morning and the world will be just as it was but for the absence of a few inconsequential bits including a white china dinner plate, and Syd thinks he will find one that looks exactly the same as that lost one, and give it to his mother for Christmas.

He could pretend it was a dream, but it wasn't: he wakes, the next morning, craving the water. He knows he will go mad, a wolfman, if he doesn't swim. Against his wishes he remembers the sight of his father stumbling onto his knees, and only the water can wash away such a hurting vision. After dinner he takes his towel and, without telling anyone, hurries up the road to the Jensons'. It is still light and will be so for a while longer, but he isn't bothered by the dark. He will tell the Jensons to ignore him, he doesn't need company or help, he will make himself as tiny an intrusion as possible: the important thing is that he swims. The hand he raises to the door is shy, but steely.

Bastian, in green pyjamas, opens the door and stares at him owlishly. "Hi, Bastian," says Syd.

"Have you come for a play?"

He proffers his towel. "No, a swim."

Bastian crinkles his nose. "I've got no one to play with."

Syd's noticed it already: the bikes aren't here. "Where's Avery and Garrick?"

"I don't know. They're not my friends. They're Colt's friends."

Syd nods. He shifts his weight. Bastian leans against the door. "So," Syd says finally. "Can I have a swim?"

Bastian smiles. "Only if you play first."

Though he could kick himself for stooping to the demands of this half-boy half-guinea-pig, Syd instantly agrees. He follows Bastian through the house, passing Mrs. Jenson in the kitchen. She is unloading a dishwasher that stands beside the sink, its sinewy pipe-arms reaching to the taps, huffing a burnt-smelling steam. "Hello, Syd," she says, and smiles her wilted smile. She always sounds tired, although she has only two children to look after, and a dishwasher.

There are worse things, he supposes, than being temporarily stuck in the playroom. The slot-car set is assembled on the floor, and it's an inviting thing. "You be blue, I'll be red," says Bastian, plumping down at the finish line with its tiny chequered flag. Syd tests the blue car's fitness by pinning it to the track and pumping the control so the car screeches and wriggles. When he lets it go it shoots off like a bullet, launching from the track and whacking into the wall. Syd smiles with brute satisfaction but Bastian cries, "Oh no, not like that!" and retrieves the car, blowing lint from its chassis. The child's idea of racing, Syd is depressed but not surprised to discover, is to have the cars travel at such a speed that they not only stay on the track, but also never outstrip each other: when he eases pressure off the control and drives the blue car slower and slower, Bastian's red car likewise slows, until they are trundling side-by-side around the course like miniature Sunday drivers in hats. "You do know what a racing car is, don't you?" he asks the child archly, and squeezes his control so the blue car powers forward, misses the corner, flies over Bastian's knees and vanishes under a bookshelf. Bastian gives a squeal and dives after it, legs flailing: truly, Syd has never met such a boy. While his host is moleishly occupied he looks longingly at the window. He can't see the swimming pool, but it's out there. He can hear the siren-call of its churning filter.

"Syd?"

He swivels on his knees: Colt stands in the doorway. "Hi."

"Is Declan here?"

"No, just me. I was going to have a swim."

"I can't find it!" Bastian complains.

A shade of disapproval crosses Colt's face. "It's pretty cold for swimming."

"I don't mind," says Syd.

"Colt!" Bastian struggles upright. "Syd made the car go under the bookshelf, and now it's lost!"

Colt crosses the room — he is not wearing pyjamas but a loose windcheater and jeans; Syd bets that one of the rules of this house is that the boys must change from their uniforms the minute they get home from school — and reaches under the bookshelf; naturally he finds the car immediately. He takes up Bastian's control and says, "I'll race you, Syd."

This is an improvement, and Syd brightens. Colt sits the cars at the starting line, Syd shuffles into a jaguar's crouch. "Ready, set, go!" says Bastian, and Syd's car rockets away, losing traction at the first bend and nose-diving into the carpet. Colt's red car zips by without a glance, negotiating the bends while humming warmly to itself, and cruises nonchalantly past the flag. "Colt wins!" Bastian declares unnecessarily, but the red car doesn't stop: it runs round and round the track, past the tennis racquets, the upturned skateboards, the soldiers on parade beside their tanks. "Slot cars aren't really about racing," Colt tells Syd.

"What are they about?"

"They're about being . . . perfect."

"Perfect." Syd blows air dismissively. "They should be about racing."

Colt nods. "They should. But they're not."

"Show him, Colt!" says Bastian.

Colt looks at Syd. "It's too late for swimming."

The idea of swimming under the stars makes Syd's blood pump fast; the thought of not swimming, now he's come this close, makes him feel a touch frantic. "I don't mind the dark. We can race another day—"

But as he speaks the doorbell rings, and the boys look in the direction of the sound. It must be Colt's father who opens the front door because they hear his voice, a rumbling purr. His footsteps press down the hall and when he stops at the door of the playroom he's in the company of Freya. "Here he is!" the man says. "The prodigal."

"Syd!" says Freya. "I told Mum you'd be here."

"It's all right," says Colt. "We've been playing with the cars."

"Colt's teaching me," Syd says quickly, indicating the track.

"But it's a school night! You're being a pest!"

Syd can see that at least half her fierceness is false, play-acting to impress Colt's father and Colt. And when the man says, "Oh, Syd's never a pest, we hardly knew he was here. And it's time well spent, racing slot cars, don't you think?" she's like a balloon popping or a flower opening up: her frown clears immediately, her hands drop from her hips. "Shall we have a cup of tea?" he asks. "Just while they finish their game? Is a cup of tea permissible on a school night?"

"Um," she says. "OK."

"I'll bring the pot out to the deck, shall I? Or would you prefer it here, in the playroom?"

She glances at the toys, the swirling racetrack, and Colt. "Um. I don't mind."

"Outside, then? It seems a shame to waste these fine evenings."

"Outside is good," she says.

When the man has gone to the kitchen, Syd asks, "Don't you want to play cars, Frey?"

"Another day," she says, and leans against the frame. "Colt's teaching you. Hi, Colt."

"Hi Freya," he says.

"Has Syd been annoying you?"

"No. We're just mucking around."

She nods and nods; and inexplicably returns to the beginning: "Don't be a pest, Syd."

Syd bites his lip against squawking that he is trying his very, very best not to be a pest, and snatches up the blue car from where it has rolled against a beanbag. Freya goes out to the deck, and through the screen door and the open louvres they hear her, dragging two of the heavy benches from beneath the outdoor table. Colt positions the cars at the starting line, takes up his control. "Look," he says, "it's all in the thumb," and brings his thumb down on the control forcefully, so the red car whizzes forward, fishtails catastrophically, and cartwheels off the track. Bastian fetches it, sets it on the line. "You have to start slowly, so you'll stay on the track; then you build up speed."

Colt's car takes off again, smoothly this time, whispering down the straight before swooping gracefully around the first noodle in the track. "It's skill," Colt says, "it's a test of skill," and they watch the red car loop the circuit one faultless lap after another. It is hypnotising, the steady pace, the mosquito burr, the confidence with which the tiny vehicle shimmies through the curves travelling neither fast nor slow but as if it has something both urgent and fragile to deliver. Colt's father passes the door carrying tea things on a tray: "How's it going in there?" he asks, but the boys don't answer and he doesn't ask again. He shoulders past the screen and they hear his strong voice. "How have you been, Freya? How's school? How's your family?"

"Good," she tells him. "The same."

"Slower into the curves, fast out of them," Colt instructs. "Even pressure on the accelerator."

Syd says, "But I want to go really fast, *all* the time."

"That doesn't work," says Colt. The boys watch the red car snake the circuit, the last little car in the world. They can hear the conversation taking place on the deck as readily as if it were being spoken in the playroom, in the centre of the track. *That brother of yours is a champ, isn't he? Petey. It seems like only yesterday my boys were his age.* To Syd, Colt says, "I guess you can either go fast all the time, and crash, and start again and have the same thing happen, go fast, crash, start again, fast, crash, start again . . . or do what works. It's one or the other."

"How is your father?" the man outside asks. "Has he been behaving?"

"Well." Freya's voice is softer, the car must go slower so it doesn't make so much noise. "Not really. I wish he wasn't rude to you at the barbeque."

"Was he rude? I don't remember that."

"It's boring," blurts Syd. "The way it works is boring —"

"If you always go fast," Colt answers quietly, "you'll always crash. It's the law."

"How's he been at home?"

"Well. You know."

Syd shifts on his knees. "There's nothing bad about crashing."

"Yeah!" says Bastian. "Crashing is fun!"

But Colt drives the car slower, so it travels at a dead crawl. Freya's voice comes past the flyscreen, the open slats, as if searching for a place to be. "We're his children, and Mum is his wife. Aren't we supposed to be his good things? But what he does . . . he doesn't seem to love us. And he doesn't seem to care if we love him or not."

"It's unfortunate." The man's voice is even, safe. "For all of you, and for him too."

"But *why* does he do it? Why is he like this? Why can't he be more like—you?"

"Be quiet, Bas," says Colt under his breath, although the boy has said nothing, and looks quizzically at his brother. They hear the bench creak as the man moves his seat. "Life is complicated, Freya," he says. "None of us go through it the way anybody else does. Who knows what history has shaped your father into being who he is? Maybe his own father was a careless man, and he grew up thinking that's how fathers must be. Maybe he has thoughts which give him trouble, make him angry, or jealous, or sad. Maybe it's none of these: maybe he just has a temper, maybe he's someone who shouldn't drink. I can't tell you, Freya. I'm not Joe. You could ask him, but you might not get an answer. He might not think there's anything wrong with the way he behaves, or maybe he'd be too ashamed to admit there is. Anyway, the only important thing to know is that you are not to blame."

"But it's *us* who suffer, not him—"

"Oh, he suffers, don't you think? He suffers. And he'll suffer more, in other ways, as time goes on."

Freya says nothing. Then, "I feel sad for him."

"Because you love him."

"It's not fair."

"No," the man says, "life isn't. But don't let that spoil it for you."

There's silence from the deck; Syd's gaze follows, as if dragged by a wheel, the tour of the red car around the track. Forgetting the command to be quiet Bastian says, "Why is your car just sitting there, Syd?" And when neither Syd nor Colt replies, he reaches for

Syd's control and sets the blue car in motion. With two engines making their insect buzz it is more difficult to hear, and Colt and Syd dip their heads.

"I don't know why they got married," says Freya. "They don't even like each other. I don't think they *ever* liked each other. They're smiling in the wedding photos, but that doesn't mean anything."

"It probably means something." The man's cup makes a sound against the table. "Maybe it means things weren't as bad as you think. You'll never know everything about your parents, Freya. No child can, just as they'll never know everything about you. Maybe they didn't have the choices you imagine they had. Sometimes people get married for reasons other than love."

"Reasons like what?"

"Well — like babies. People sometimes get married because of babies."

Again there's silence on the deck, or at least nothing Syd can hear. Then something startling: "I don't know for sure, but I think Mum's having a baby."

"That's wonderful. Babies are lovely."

"No they're not. We haven't got anywhere to put another baby. We haven't got enough money for another baby. We don't need another baby. I wish Mum would stop having babies!"

There's a throaty chuckle, although Syd sees no reason for laughter. He can hear the distress in his sister, and suffers waves of distress himself. "Once again," says Colt's father, in his voice that knows everything, "maybe your mother doesn't have the choices you think she does."

Freya says, "I don't know what I think, but I know she's got enough kids already!"

"Maybe she needs you," says the man.

"What?" Syd hears her scowl. "What do you mean?"

"Well, maybe you're her—how did you put it, a moment ago? *Good things*. Maybe you're her good things."

"You can have too many good things," says Freya.

"Can you?" says the man. "I'm not sure about that."

Bastian has completely lost patience with his brother and friend; as the cars amble past he karate-chops them off the track. Colt says dumbly, "You crashed them."

"I crashed them!" Bastian agrees stormily. "You've played enough!"

Syd can't look up from the floor; he feels a nauseating sense of exposure, as if they've caught him with a finger up his nose. Abruptly he scrabbles to his feet and shouts, "Freya! We can go home now!"

Colt picks up the cars and sits them on the track. "It's all right," he says. "Nothing's broken."

Syd hears this and desperately needs it to be true; he can't have the conversation cost him the BMX, the playroom, the water. He feels himself pouting, being swept down a drain. "It's a school night," he says. "We have to go home."

The red car resumes its stately tour around the curves, along the straights, past the finish line and onwards. "Come back on the weekend," Colt says. "We can race again. Now you've learned something."

Syd looks at him blindly, and cannot speak: “Freya!” he barks at the window, “hurry up!” And then his sister is at the door: “All right!” she says. “Don’t yell! Jeez.”

They walk home together, Syd with his towel around his shoulders, his mind racing like a rabbit in a paddock. The sky is darker, and streetlights have come on. “Why did you tell that man those things?” he asks, because he’s always believed — although he can’t remember being taught — that what happens in their house on his father’s bad nights is something they are supposed to keep to themselves. His mother never says much about it afterwards, and Syd’s uncles and aunt and grandparents don’t say anything either. Even between themselves, his brothers and sisters, it is not something they discuss. On the mornings after even the worst nights they get up and get dressed, eat breakfast, go to school, and though memories move through Syd like a virus as he assumes they move through his siblings too, no one mentions it, they drive it down. And the reason is that it’s embarrassing: it’s *embarrassing* to have a father who cares so little about them, it’s *shameful* that their family isn’t happy. No one must know: and now somebody does. “Isn’t it — the secret?” he asks.

Freya is walking fast, so he has to hurry. She is much taller than he is, to the degree that he’s sure he will never catch up. All his life he’s had the greatest respect for her, his infinitely smarter sister, as well as a healthy dose of caution; and he is not so much angry at her as impressed that she could so casually break something he’d believed was ironclad. He thinks she’s about to introduce him to a world where the rules are much looser than those which bind him, and he's ready, he's thrilled: so it's disappointing when she says, "It *is* a secret. Don't go telling everyone."

"But you told *him*—"

"It's a secret," she says, and he hears her teeth grit, "but not a secret from him. Is that OK, Your Highness? Is that all right with you?"

A pinch or some other asp-like act of violence is close; Syd steps sideways, and doesn't say no.

Avery Price rides his bike at night, around the cricket oval, across the schoolyard, down to the creek, up to the milkbar, and much further afield: past the shops grouped at the tram terminus, along the supermarket carpark, to the train station and the offramp of the freeway, to many places he doesn't need to go. His bicycle carries him easily, he will journey for hours, sometimes two or three hours or more, through the blackest quietest hours of the night. He rides in the centre of the vacant roads, the streetlights repeatedly finding him and letting him go, occasionally swerving onto the footpath where the darkness is thicker and where he finds objects of interest that have slipped free from the daytime world: car keys, a glove, a letter that never reached the mailbox. The wheels of his bike make a steady unzipping sound as they whirl. If he sees people on the street farewelling friends or arguing or smoking against a fence, he changes direction without hesitation and speeds away. He often encounters dogs who've been released into the night and they ramble alongside him for a while, their tongues lightly swinging; he sees cats sprinting over the road or standing, arch-spined, on fences, eyes locked on the face of their foe.

Avery loves these night rides more than anything else he knows. He loves the damp breeze skimming past him, the sound of the tyres on tarmac, the brotherhood of the animals. He loves his bike, his reliable friend. When he cruises around the midnight streets he is the captain of his life, carefree. The sights to which he has been the sole witness are innumerable. The hours he's pedalled through make a dark palace into which he retreats when his teachers berate him, when his sister slams her door, when he imagines what's coming and sees nothing.

Lately he has been thinking about Garrick, who is and always has been a kind of beloved enemy of Avery Price. Garrick insists he is superior to Avery, but everyone knows he is not — even Garrick, *especially* Garrick. They know each other well, these boys from the bottom of the pile; only Garrick bothers pretending that the bottom is the top.

He thinks about Garrick, and Garrick's behaviour of late, which has not been very different from the usual — he's still Garrick; the word makes Avery think of a black mole on the skin — yet there is something strange. Around Colt Jenson, Garrick is changed, but it's tricky for Avery to say how. It is as if there is something inside Garrick which cannot rest unless it's looking at Colt, or forcing Colt to look at it.

Saturday is a momentous day: the bandage comes off his leg. It's been nearly two weeks and under Mr. Jenson's care the wound, which had been dreadful, is as neat and clean as a porcelain pin tray. The flesh is sealed with a pale scab, tender and slick in the centre, leathery at the edges. His calf is criss-crossed with greasy remnants of the sticking-plaster. Mr. Jenson licks his thumb and rubs futilely at these. "You need a good soaking," he says.

The injury has taken up too much space in his life; it's a relief to be free of the burden of trying to care about it as much as Mr. Jenson does. Avery doesn't want to flee the clutches of the Jenson household — a street cat of a boy, he's found good and plentiful food there, warm rooms full of wonders — but he is used to looking after himself, to judging the depth of his own danger. He's used to the freedom of neglect; he likes it.

He's an agile daredevil, a quick learner of every mischievous skill, and flies down the Jensons' driveway on the striped skateboard so fast that Bastian howls. Speed carries him over the gutter, the board soaring as it hits the dip. At first he can't manage it and has to leap for his life: three attempts later he has the hang of it, knows exactly how to distribute his weight and absorb the wallop of the landing. Bastian's shrieking brings Mrs. Jenson to the porch. "Avery!" she calls, "you'll be hit by a car! You'll be killed!" And Avery smiles through the trees to her: he won't get hit by a car.

The boys play together into the afternoon; Avery knows that his friends spurn Bastian Jenson, but Avery doesn't mind him. They are suited to the company of each other, neither of them mean-spirited, both content to while away the day with the mildest amusement. When Garrick appears on the crest of the afternoon he has with him two fat green sticks of bubblegum which, bitten, bleed a sweet pink fluid. One stick has been ravaged, its wrapper shredded away, the gum protruding like the diseased shinbone of a zombie. Garrick plumps down on the naturestrip between Avery and Bastian, chewing loudly. “What are you spazzos doing?”

“Nothing. Sitting.”

“Sitting here like little birdies. Two little turdy birdies.” He chews and chews, black eyes staring across the road, his jaw working methodically. “Where’s Colt?” he asks, as Avery has known he would.

“Out with Dad,” says Bastian, proud keeper of all facts about his brother.

“Out where?”

“Out at the shops.”

“Doing what?”

Even to Bastian the question is silly. “Buying things!”

“When will he be back?”

The boy shrugs. “Probably later.”

Garrick rolls his eyes. Chomp, chomp, chomp. “This tastes like shit,” he says, plucking the glistening wodge from his mouth and hurling it mightily into bushes on the far side of the road. He’s stronger than a boy his age needs to be. He tosses the packets of gum into the gutter as if he never cared about them in the first place. “This is shit,” he says. “I’m bored with this shit. Let’s go somewhere. The pinballs.”

“Nah,” says Avery.

“Get the BMX out, then. Why are you just sitting here?”

“We like sitting here,” says Bastian.

“You don’t have to,” says Avery.

Garrick sneers savagely. “Homos.” Only then does he notice Avery’s knee, released at last from its swaddling. The scab is interesting — its centre is weirdly translucent, it is possible to imagine strange fish swimming under there — and he asks, “Leggy-weggy all fixed now, is it?”

“Just about.”

Garrick’s lightless gaze lingers on Avery’s eyes, something like a smile on his face. “Did you get a kiss to make it better?”

“. . . No.”

“Are you sure?” Garrick lifts a hand and strokes it heavily down Avery’s head. “Sure you don’t need a kiss? For your poor little bleeding knee-wee?”

Avery shakes away his touch. “Piss off.”

“Piss off? Oh, now you’ve hurt my feelings. I only want to help you, Avery. I want to take care of you. You’re so small and skinny and helpless. You smell so nice I could eat you. I want to stroke your hair and your lovely skin —”

He grabs for Avery’s ribcage, and Avery struggles. “Get off!”

“But Avery, I love you!”

Bastian, laughing throatily, says, “He loves you, Avery!”

“Just one kiss, that’s all I want!”

“Kiss him, Avery!”

“Just a peck! One on the lips! After all I’ve done for you!”

Avery springs up, spinning away. For an instant he seems about to bolt, a bird taking to the sky. Instead he reels on the road to the giggling boy. “Don’t laugh at him, Bastian!” he barks.

Bastian swallows his laughter like a rock. Garrick leans on his palms, grinning loosely. “Hey, Bastian,” he says. “Do you like living here now?”

Bastian turns to him eagerly. “I do like it.”

“What about the bogeyman? Do you like him too?”

Bastian’s downy eyebrows dive. “What bogeyman? Is there a bogeyman?”

“Yeah! If you listen really hard, you can hear him. *Bastian! Bastian! Come to me, little boy!*”

He crooks a finger, beckoning: Bastian shrinks back in the grass. “There’s no such thing as a bogeyman.”

“There is,” Garrick says. “I’ve seen him.”

From the centre of the road Avery says, “Shut up, Garrick. You’re an idiot.”

“What does he look like?” asks Bastian.

“Well, you know. Like a normal person. Like a good guy who’s actually a bad guy.”

Bastian thinks on this. “Where does he live?”

“Pretty close. Really close. He’s probably watching us.”

“It’s not true,” says Avery. “Ignore him, Bastian. He’s full of shit.”

“Yeah, just ignore me,” Garrick agrees. “I talk about things they don’t want you to know. Like about the bogeyman. And about . . .”

“About what?”

“Oh, about—you know. The creepy-crawlies. The ones who live in the trees and in the stormwater drain and under your house. They’ve got big green fangs and rusty nails for fingers, and they love to eat little boys. Can you hear that noise?”

"What noise?"

"Listen—it sounds like the wind blowing, or cars driving past. That's the creepy-crawlies talking to each other. They sound like something ordinary, but they're not. They're ugly stinking creepy-crawlies who should be killed. And you know which one is the scariest?"

"Which one?"

"Me!" blares Garrick, and Bastian leaps to his feet and runs up the driveway, hands flapping, screaming like a parrot, a boy born for this world only if the world is a stage. Avery, watching him go, grumbles. "We'll be in trouble now." But the minutes pass and no one comes out to scold them, and soon Bastian's face appears at the window half-wary, shyly grinning, and when he sees that Avery and Garrick are still sitting on the naturestrip he makes a bold return to the street. "You're not a creepy-crawly!" he cries, jabbing a finger at Garrick, and Garrick says, "Nah, I'm only a person. There's only people, isn't there?"

Later, when the afternoon is closing down and the neighbourhood boys have gone home and Colt is in the kitchen making peanut-butter toast, Bastian asks him, just to be certain, "There's no creepy-crawlies who eat kids, are there? Garrick said they live under our house."

"No, that's not true," says Colt.

"What about the bogeyman? Garrick says he's watching us."

Colt lifts his head to look at his brother. "You're not stupid," he tells him. "Don't believe stupid stories."

And sometimes he does try to convince himself there is no such thing as the bogeyman — that he's imagining things which don't exist, looking at them from the wrong angle, hearing them with a mistaken tone. That the fault is his own. But when he tries to talk himself into seeing things in this simpler, infinitely preferable way, he feels his existence thin. He cannot tell lies to himself. His mother is fighting the same battle as he is — he sees it in her eyes, where it moves like clouds — and he understands that she is losing: despite the set of her mouth and the muffled conversations at night, she is losing. He walks into the depths of the stormwater drain, puzzling on this. She's no fool, his mother. And her husband, Colt reasons, is the pillar of her life. He's the money, the house, the schooling, the meals. He's the shirts on their backs and the boots on their feet. They need him to hold up the ceiling. His wife can lose faith in him, but she cannot lose *him,* because then there'll be no roof over her sons. So she's pushing it down, pushing herself down, not blinding but certainly dulling her eyes for the sake of her children. Colt leans against the flank of the pipe, sliding gradually down into the thread of slime. It cannot be easy, and he wonders how she finds the courage to do it — to unknow what she knows, and to do it for her children. To let them take the heavy tail-end of the blame.

The weather is clear although not hot on Sunday, but Declan, Syd and Avery don't mind swimming in such weather. Colt has no choice but to join them. There are various toys that Colt's father has bought — a beachball, a lilo, a swag of gigantic blow-up baseball bats — and the boys plunge through the water with these. The water is cold, and as blue as the sky it reflects; as the boys haul about, it slops over the edge in great slurpy swathes to splatter the ground below, which Rex has now concreted with pavers to prevent mud tracking into the pool and the house. The water lashes at the boys' smooth backs and naked chests, reaches knifelike for their throats. Colt's blood is warmed beneath his chill skin. They invent a game which involves bats and territory, and soon there is an exhaustion in him that he recognises from when he used to run around a track, a spentness that is borne like a bearskin while beneath it the muscles, blood and heart itself grow powerful and weightless. There are moments when Colt feels he could jump mountains; that he's strong enough, when he is happy, to escape the very clutches of time and space.

Then Rex arrives home from wherever he has been. "What's going on here?" he asks, grinning from the steps of the deck, and Colt's heart sinks through the water to the rocks at the earth's core. "Avery, how's your knee?" The boys wave and say, "Hi, Mr. Jenson," and Colt's father repeats his threadbare line and Colt would like to leap from the pool and swing at him not with one of the blow-up bats but with the real one propped in the corner of the playroom, a hard expensive piece of equipment given to him although he's never had an interest in baseball, never learned to play, never lived near a diamond, never watched a game on TV. Given to him in case he made a friend who loved the game. *Mr. Jenson is my father. Call me Rex.* "Syd," Rex asks, "are you drowning? Don't drown, whatever you do. Your mother wouldn't be pleased. How's the temperature in there? You all look a bit blue around the gills."

Colt says, "We're OK, Dad, don't worry."

"I'm not worried. I'm just wondering if I'll be able to chip ice off you for my drink."

The boys laugh as they are meant to; Colt turns away. The water chops and roils, he's speckled with goosebumps. He expects the visitors to have lost interest in playing, as he himself no longer cares — but Syd gives a shout and brings his bat down on Avery's head, and suddenly the air is billowing under the boofy swing of the bats. And Colt, beaten against the pool's wall, wants to order them to stop, to realise what they are doing, that this is what he's come to see so they should not show it to him: but it's an impossible thing to say. It might not be true. And if it is true, it is impossible to say. And for an instant he sees his mother's reticence in a different light. It is simply unutterable.

He feels his father's gaze on his spine; Colt must have the hearing of a dog, because below his friends' laughter he hears his father light one of his rare cigarettes. He fears he will hear each indrawn breath, every crackle of the cigarette paper, the shrivel of the tobacco as it burns. He'll hear the smoke travel down the tube of his father's windpipe and swill inside his lungs, he'll hear it gust up the gullet and out the smiling mouth to be emitted, stale and shapeless, into the day. "Stop!" he says, dropping his bat. "I need to stop—"

Declan shoulders his own bat. "You feel sick?"

Colt shakes his head: *sick* isn't the word. He wants a word which describes the desire to climb to the top of a tree and stay there. "It's too cold," he says. "I'm getting out." But when he works through the water and climbs down the ladder and finally looks to where his father is standing, his father isn't there, there's no ash on the deck, no smoky scent on the air. Nevertheless, he feels frozen solid. He takes his towel and rubs his face and arms but he's colder than he's ever been in his life. His father was right, he is as blue as if he's absorbed the sky's reflection, donned the most torturous camouflage. His bathers cling to his shanks and his jaw judders: if he stands here half-naked he will die, but he hardly dares leave. "I'll be back," he calls out, "in one minute." In his bedroom he dresses as quickly as his frigid limbs allow, working socks painfully over his feet. He can't hear Bastian or his mother, and doesn't know where they are. He can't hear his father either—it is as if Colt dreamed of him. From outside comes the sound of boys' voices but his dog-hearing has finished, he can't make out what they say. When he's pulled on enough clothes he hurries back through the house feeling marginally repaired—and stops just inside the screen door, invisible behind the flywire mesh, because the boys have climbed out of the pool and are standing, dripping, on the deck, which preserves a pattern of their wet footprints, their irregular, pattering feet. And Colt's father is there, materialised from nowhere, handing out towels and laughing, as if only laughter will keep the planet turning. "Look at you!" he's saying. "You're as white as driven snow. How are you, Avery? Let me see that knee."

But it is the boy's fragile head that he takes in his towel-draped hands, scrubbing the cloth so roughly into the blond hair that Avery staggers sideways and Rex must grab him by the forearm saying, "Whoops there, hold still." He runs the towel over the boy's throat and shoulders and ribcage, the job done so efficiently it's like watching a man who loathes what he's doing but can never stop doing it or thinking about doing it; he crouches and dries Avery's legs, first the outside then the inside, around the ankles, over the knees, up the childish thighs. Then, with a flourish, he wraps the towel round the boy's waist, tucking in the corner with a poke of two long fingers. "Better?" he asks, and reaches out to brush strands of hair from Avery's eyes. "Good lad," he says. Then he turns to the Kiley brothers, who have been drying themselves druggily while watching this spectacle, and asks, "Who's next?"

"Oh," says Declan, laughing a little, in a voice that doesn't want to touch the ground. "It's all right, Mr. Jenson—"

"Your hair is soaking, Syd. You might catch pneumonia!"

Syd shakes his head rapidly. "No, I won't—"

"Look, come here. I can't stand seeing a boy with wet hair."

And before Syd can flee he is captured, pulled forward, and Rex scruffs the towel so crazily over his head that it's as if cats are fighting under there, and Syd squawks and his hands come up, flying as wildly as the towel. This is a joke, Rex is chortling, this is fun fun fun. "Are you dry now?" he asks, and Syd cries, "Yes!" And Rex says louder, "What's that? I can't hear you! Are you under there, Syd?" and Syd wails, "Yes, I'm here, I'm dry!" But the towel resumes its insane whirling and the boy beneath it veers drunkenly left and right. Rex says, "Syd Kiley! Are you alive? Where have you gone, Syd?" And Syd, with what's left of his strength, bawls, "I'm dry! I am! You can stop!"

Rex pulls the towel from Syd's head and squints at him innocently. "There you are! We've been looking for you. How on earth did your hair get so messy?"

He steps back smirking, very pleased with the boy, who lurches off dizzily. He looks, then, at Declan. "You need some drying, bucko?"

"No, I'm OK . . ."

"You sure?"

Declan is reversing, towel clutched to his body. He backs into the railing and stops. "I'm dry. I promise."

"Hmm." Colt's father eyes him. "Bone-dry," he says.

"You nearly dried my face off," says Syd.

Rex spins, plants a hand on Syd's shoulder. "I think there are party pies in the freezer. Shall I put them in the oven?"

And as his father strides for the screen door Colt steps into the playroom, pressing his back to the wall. He hears his father go to the kitchen, and the pop of the freezer opening. Through the louvres he hears his friends — they are not talking, but they are laughing, snuffling in a furtive way which makes Colt think of the boys at school who, when the teacher's back is turned, do whip-quick, cruelly brilliant imitations of that teacher while the other boys smother their giggling. He hears his father moving around the kitchen, filling glasses with Passiona and dollops of ice-cream. He hears Declan, Avery and Syd shushing each other. And Colt tries to tell himself that it's nothing, nothing, if they're laughing it can't be bad, if they're laughing he is imagining it and it's not his father who is at fault but only he, himself, Colt, seeing and hearing and thinking everything wrong. But it's thin as paper, this line. Hands to his face, he prays for the floor to swallow him; he wouldn't care, he'd go gladly. They would look for him and find absolutely nothing. He doesn't want to stand up straight, doesn't know if he'll be able to stay standing once he's up. But his father is calling from the kitchen, "Who wants a Passiona spider?" and the boys are pulling open the screen door, and Colt is on his feet before he knows it, moving swiftly, galvanised.

Freya finds she's thought of something curious. She burrows into the grass and the stringy shadows beneath the clothesline and asks, "Why did you and Dad get married?"

Her mother is hanging the washing—she has a systematic way of doing so, socks pegged at the mouth, trousers by the cuffs, dresses at the hem, shirts open so their empty arms reach beseechingly for the ground. Freya knows it causes her mother real anguish to see clothes hung another way. It's a sunny afternoon but Elizabeth does the laundry on every day that isn't determinedly raining. "Oh," she answers airily, "I can't remember. It was a long time ago."

But Freya knows it wasn't so long ago. She is nearly thirteen, so thirteen years is a lifetime to her: but she knows her parents bought this house—her white weatherboard house—soon after they got married, not long before Freya was born. Not much more than thirteen years ago. She lies with her nose level with the spikes of the grass, watching her mother bow to the washing basket, choose a garment—one of Joe's shirts—to suit the available length of clothesline, pluck three pegs from the tin—always three pegs for a shirt—and hang the shirt with heron-like jabs at the line, tweaking it when she's finished so the sleeves open, the collar jerks straight. "I suppose I wanted to marry him," Elizabeth says, bending again. "I must have liked him."

"You *suppose*?"

"Yes," she says testily, "I suppose."

Freya watches her. She can be standoffish and quick-tempered, her mother, known to laugh at her serious, fussy, equally quick-tempered daughter. But Freya refuses to be deterred: she has a right to answers. There's something hard at her elbow, and she prises a peg from the dirt. It's faded and snaggle-toothed, a tiny blue crocodile. "Was it because . . ." She pauses, making the crocodile bite. "Was it because of babies?"

Her mother looks at her, and Freya's gaze skids away: it has always been difficult for her to meet her mother's eye. In many ways, she thinks, they are strangers. Freya was born, and fast after her came Declan and Syd, and by the time Marigold arrived Freya had shouldered the responsibility of raising herself. She is often called on to help with the children, her mother expecting her to be capable, which she is—but Elizabeth doesn't keep track of Freya, she doesn't know what her daughter wants or worries about, and she has no time to find out. And that's understandable, Freya accepts it. If she is nervous at the prospect of making her way alone through what awaits her, she also knows that she has courage. She knows, too, that her mother's advice wouldn't necessarily be the best advice. She, Freya, does not want to spend her life doing laundry.

“Because of babies?” her mother echoes. “Everyone had babies in those days.”

“But is it why you married Dad?” Freya presses. “Because of babies? Did you want them? Did Dad want them? Or did you only want them because everyone else had them?”

Her mother is easily made cross: she swats Declan’s jeans with the back of a hand. ”Oh, I don’t know,” she says. “You’re like a dog with a bone, Freya. I married him because I wanted to marry him, that’s why. He was nice-looking. He was a good dancer. All the girls liked him.”

Freya can’t ask, *But did* you *like him—did you love him?* because she would choke on the words, love being something never mentioned in the Kiley household, their conversations all being about food and television and Declan’s football timetable and whether Marigold can have a pet mouse. Never the kind of conversation Freya’s had with Rex Jenson on the deck. And even if she could find a way to ask, her mother might answer that no, she never loved him, or that she thought she did and found out too late that she didn’t. It is dangerous to ask questions, Freya sees. And, spooked, she would let the subject die if not for Elizabeth saying curtly, “You don’t need a man to be happy,” which makes her daughter look up and say, “What?”

Her mother is poking through the tin as if somewhere in its depths is the most important peg of all; she’s frowning, irritated. “Never think you have to have a man in your life,” she says without looking up. “You don’t. They make you think you do, but you don’t. I was too dumb to know better, back then.”

Freya is astonished to hear this; and afraid. "What about kids?" she asks. "Do you need them?"

"Kids are nothing but a worry," her mother replies. "You worry about them from the moment they're born. No, never have children, Freya."

Freya feels shocked, almost bamboozled. "But Mum," she says, "aren't we—good things?"

Elizabeth straightens to the clothes hoist and spins it expertly, so the clothes flap like dank wings around her. "Sometimes you're all right," she says.

Freya considers her in silence, struggling to understand the moment she is living through. She knows her mother loves her, and that she's only ever rough because it's easier and quicker than being smooth; still, she wishes they could talk properly, like proper people do. If they could talk properly, Freya might ask, now they're speaking of such things, if there's to be a baby; yet she's also unsure if she wants to know. She lingers while her mother hangs a few more clothes, then gets up and walks into the house. She has been putting this off, but now is the time.

In the lounge there is a sideboard, and in the sideboard's cupboard are the family photo albums. Freya loves the albums, and knows every photograph in detail: she can identify each bald baby even when its own mother cannot. It has been Elizabeth's sole extravagance, the photographing of her children as they've grown. The pictures are a luxury, and Joe resents the expense, so Elizabeth tries to save money by crowding into each photograph as many children as will fit. And here they are, the Kiley offspring in shades of black and white and, more recently, in muted colours that make the photographed world look rather rancid. They're holding kittens, dressed for parties, standing in a row under the pine tree in the yard, crowding around the big pram, sitting at a miniature table on miniature chairs. Here they are at the zoo, the beach, under sprinklers, squeezing dough, posing in oversized uniforms on the first day of school. Freya is photographed as frequently as her siblings, her hair growing longer and darkening from white to fawn, her face growing thinner, gradually beginning to lose the race to stay taller than Declan. She's the girl holding Dorrie's toddler hand, hoisting the newborn Peter. There she is, nine years old, astride the purple bike she was given for her birthday, its rear wheel fanned by the elastic strings of the skirt-guard. She used to ride it often, but rarely does anymore. She is growing up, there will be no more photos of her rat-haired and grinning from running under the sprinkler.

At the front of the album are the wedding pictures — only three, but each is large enough to take up an entire page of the album, and they're printed on thick paper with the signature of the photographer looped across a corner. Her mother and father stand at the doors of the church, freshly married when the shutter snapped, his suited arm around her ivory waist, and although there must have been guests at the wedding — friends, bridesmaids, Elizabeth's parents and brothers, Joe's older sister — they stand alone, a pair, looking at the camera as if it has something to say to them. It's difficult for Freya to decide if her mother is right — if Joe is handsome. He looks well-groomed, amused around the eyes.

Elizabeth is wearing pearls at her throat and in her hair. More than anything, they are young. Freya looks at them, looks past them into their future of the weatherboard house, the rowdy children, the washing basket, the printing machines. Thirteen years ago, her parents knew nothing about this world that awaited them; Freya has never known anything else. If she had been there, a guest at her parents' wedding, she wonders what she would have told them. You don't need a man, never have children, you will regret this, the heart is wicked above all things.

With great care she prises the first photograph from the album, mindful of bending or tearing it. Her mother's habit is to write, on the flipside of each image, the name and age of those pictured, as well as the location and date. It's a habit that fills a couple of hours each time an envelope of prints comes back from the chemist, but Elizabeth swears it must be done or else she'll forget everything of which the photograph is meant to remind her. And sure enough there is her handwriting on the flipside of the photograph, recording her age and Joe's age and, as Freya has known it would, the date. She stares at it glassily for a time, and around her the house breathes and goes on. The schoolbags, the cups in the sink, the volume knob on the television. The station wagon in the driveway, the branches stacked behind the garage, the holes in the fibro walls of the shed. The swing near the back fence hanging from its steel frame, a long leg of which javelins out of the ground if the swing is swung very high and forcefully. Her mother, who has moved into the kitchen to cobble together a dinner over which the children will moan. Sometimes, if their behaviour at the table is particularly deplorable, she will take her plate and go to eat in her bedroom. Probably she's glad of the excuse for some peace, but her departure always makes Freya feel as grey as a gravestone.

She smooths the photograph into place fastidiously, and drapes the plastic sheet down on top of it. Then she slides the album into the sideboard and closes the cupboard with barely a sound.

Syd has been to the milkbar to get the milk and when he arrives home, after a longer-than-necessary journey, dinner is being served in the kitchen. He puts the milk in the fridge and takes his place opposite Declan and beside Marigold, a corner seat with his shoulders to the wall. They have a plain wooden set of table and chairs, and Syd likes this furniture very much. He likes it when supermarket bags are sprawled across the table's waxy surface, he likes it when tea-towels, hung to dry over the backs of the chairs, go stiff enough to stand up on their own. Tonight's dinner is something the children adore, sausage casserole with rice and beans. Their mother is always scrupulously fair about quantity and quality. No child likes to see another receiving more or better than themselves. Declan is her favourite, they all agree about that; it doesn't mean he can be better fed than the lesser lights.

Syd drops into his seat saying, "When I went past the Jensons' I saw Avery and Garrick on the BMX. Garrick was pedalling and Avery was riding on the handlebars."

"That boy is not long for this world," says Elizabeth.

"I hate Garrick," says Marigold.

"You hate everyone," says Dorrie.

"Yeah." Marigold sighs.

Peter is sitting in his highchair, which he loathes. He wants a proper chair, the same as his siblings; already he is wasting his life trying to catch up to them. He squirms and says, "Let me out!" and Declan, reaching over to stuff him back behind the tray, asks, "Where was Colt?"

"I didn't see him. Or Bastian."

"The person I hate the most is Avery's grandpa." It's Tuesday, and Marigold is still wearing her school uniform, a dress dappled blue and white and stained down the buttons with orange cordial. "I bet Avery would rather fall off the handlebars and die, than live with that mean old man forever."

"You don't even know Avery's grandfather," says Syd.

"We know him," says Dorrie mysteriously.

"Yeah. He walks past the house and we see him. He looks at us."

"He should mind his own business," says Dorrie. "Old coot."

"Don't say that, Dorrie." Their mother ladles casserole onto a plate, piles up rice and beans around it, and sets the plate aside. This is their father's dinner, and the children know not to touch it. They don't know where their father is, and they don't remark on his absence. Now he thinks of it, Syd can't remember his father ever eating at the table with them — which is good, because there's not enough space for another chair. When their mother takes her seat they are allowed to start eating. "That's not a nice thing to say," Elizabeth tells her youngest daughter.

"He *should* mind his own business, though." Marigold shakes the soy-sauce bottle over her rice, sprinkling a black rain. "Me and Dorrie were outside today, and we were playing, and Avery's grandpa came past, I think he was taking a letter to the box, and he looked at us, and then he stuck his nose in our business."

"What did he do?"

"Well, we were pretending that Dorrie was a puppy, so she had a leash — it was one of Dad's belts. And Avery's grandpa told us to take the leash off because it was dangerous. And it wasn't dangerous! Dorrie wasn't even hurt."

Dorrie lifts her little pie of a face and smiles. "See?"

"But we took it off," continues Marigold, shovelling black rice onto her fork, "and when he'd gone I put it back on, because Dorrie had to have the leash, that was part of the game. And then a few minutes later he walks past again and says, *What did I tell you? Take that rope off* — it wasn't even a rope! It was Dad's belt! — *before that child is killed!*"

"So what did you do?"

Marigold's hands fling out, spilling rice on Syd and the floor. "We came inside! We had to. He spoiled everything."

Their mother asks, "Where was the belt tied on Dorrie?"

It's the question on which everything hinges, including the indignation on Marigold's face, which sets stonily. "It was around her neck," she admits. "But it wasn't tight! She was being a puppy! She had to have a leash. She wasn't choking —"

Dorrie makes a gagging sound, and Peter copies her, and Marigold rolls her eyes. "She *wasn't* choking. We were just playing.

And it wasn't that old man's business. He shouldn't talk to us. He doesn't know us. I hate him. And I bet Avery hates him."

"He doesn't," says Declan.

"Avery loves everyone," says Dorrie.

"You're just mad because Mr. Price wouldn't let you strangle Dorrie with Dad's belt," says Syd.

"No," says Marigold, "I'm mad because he *doesn't* care about Avery, but he *does* care about Dorrie."

"Avery's mum should look after him," says Dorrie. "Not the old coot."

"Eat your dinner and stop saying that," says their mother.

Marigold spears a wedge of pineapple sullenly. "When can we put up the Christmas tree?" she asks. "Tonight? Tomorrow?"

The calendar has finally turned to its last page, an occasion of much excitement for the younger Kileys: the treasures on their wishlists suddenly seem within grasp. But, "Not yet," says Elizabeth. "Wait a few more days."

"Ah! Why?"

"It's too early for the tree."

"But it says Christmas on the calendar!"

"No, Marigold."

"Why not? Why? Why? Why? Why?"

"Marigold," says Freya crisply, "Mum said no."

Marigold slumps, lip jutting. "What are you getting from Santa?" Declan asks Dorrie.

Dorrie sits up straight and announces, "A crown."

"Like a queen," explains Marigold tiredly. "I already told you: you can't have a crown, because you can't buy them in shops. You can only have something you can buy."

"There are crown shops," says Dorrie.

"You can only have a crown if you're a princess," says Declan.

"No," says Dorrie. "I saw a lady with a crown, and she wasn't a princess."

"That's another fib," says Marigold.

During this inane conversation Syd has been working steadily through his dinner, and now he folds his knife and fork. "Can I please leave the table?"

Normally he would hang about for leftovers, and certainly in the hope of dessert. They know there is neopolitan ice-cream in the freezer, the chocolate section gouged away, the strawberry likewise almost gone, only the vanilla remaining intact, a snowy wall standing in the centre of the vat. "Why?" asks their mother. "Where are you rushing off to?"

Syd pauses to frame it correctly. "I want to ride the BMX. I know it's a school night, I won't stay out late—"

"No," says Declan.

It's unexpected, and Syd frowns across the table. "Why not?"

Declan doesn't look up from his plate. "Don't go by yourself."

"Then come with me . . ."

"I've got homework."

Elizabeth is looking at Declan. "Why shouldn't he go there by himself?"

"It's night-time," says Dorrie. "Scary."

Declan crinkles his nose as if he has unearthed something unidentifiable in his dinner. "He's just a bit strange, Mr. Jenson."

"What? He is not!" says Freya.

"Strange how?" asks Marigold. "Strange like an alien? Remember you said he was an alien, Freya?"

"Shut up!" says Freya.

"He's OK," says Syd. "You've just got to keep away from him, that's all." He smiles, and his fingers stroke the air like insect legs, and Declan snickers.

Elizabeth frowns down the table at her sons. "What are you talking about? Declan?"

"Nothing." Declan sits back grinning, although his cheeks are stained faintly pink. "He's all right. He just likes giving shoulder rubs. Patting your back, stuff like that."

"You gotta stay out of reach," reiterates Syd, and his fingers paw the air, and Declan chortles again.

Freya is staring icily at her brothers. "Don't be mean. That's really mean. Mr. Jenson is kind. He bought us ice-cream. Why do you have to be so horrible?"

"We're not being horrible, it's just funny—"

"I've talked to him lots of times, I've sat next to him, and he's never rubbed my shoulders or patted my back. I've never seen him do that to anyone."

Declan looks at her, still smiling, and suddenly his face goes bright: "You saw him do it to Syd!"

"When?"

"At the barbeque! When we were leaving, when Syd wouldn't get out of the pool."

The whole family looks at Freya, even Peter, who is licking rice off his palm. Freya shakes her head. "He helped Syd get dry!"

"Yeah—"

"We were going home. Everyone was waiting. He got Syd dry. He rubbed him with a towel. That's how you dry someone." She impales her brother on a glare. "What's so bad about that?"

"Syd's not a baby," says Marigold. "He can dry himself."

"He'd been told ten times to get out of the pool. We couldn't wait for him all night!"

Declan considers his sister, then looks away and says, "Don't worry about it."

"We're just used to Dad." Freya speaks darkly. "Mr. Jenson isn't Dad. He likes everyone. He isn't nasty—"

"Dad's not nasty!" yikes Dorrie.

"—and you shouldn't say nasty things about him. So what if he pats you on the back? That's called *being nice.*"

Declan is not a boy for fighting lost causes, but, "It's still weird," he says.

"Alien," says Marigold.

Freya wheels on her sister. "If you say that again I will smash you, Marigold!"

Elizabeth pushes her chair out and turns to the stove, and stirs the casserole more than it needs—as if, for a moment, she can't stop stirring it. "There's a bit of leftover," she says. "Does anyone want some?"

"I bags!" says Marigold.

To Syd, Declan shakes his head. "Don't go."

Freya snarls, "Ignore him, Syd!"

But Syd, although he's childishly torn, has a businessman's instinct for erring on the side that is most beneficial to him, and stays resignedly in his chair.

Their father is home late but he hasn't been drinking, Syd can tell by the sound of his footsteps and because his mother asks, "How are you?" which she wouldn't if he didn't deserve the question. The children are in bed but Syd isn't close to sleeping. Since Christmas appeared on the calendar he has become more restless than usual. Now that he's discovered the pleasure of a private swimming pool he'd like to have one of his own: given the unlikelihood of this happening, he's staked all his hopes on a skateboard. He needs a skateboard. He has told his school friends that he'll be getting a skateboard, so it's more than imperative: the quality of his future hangs on the ownership of a skateboard. And every atom of his being has begun to tingle in fear that his wish will not come true.

He sees the skateboards at the Jenson house, propped against the wall of the playroom, both as good as new. Neither Colt nor Bastian knows how lucky they are to have them; Syd feels, as if it were manacles on his wrists, the ponderous unfairness of it. He detests being poor. From the chocolate biscuits he won't eat for afternoon tea to the lessons in gymnastics in which he'll only ever imagine excelling, Syd is already weary, at ten, of the constant deprivation that is the lack of money. He lies in bed, curled on his side, listening to Declan's sleep-breathing, envisaging for himself a life in which he will own everything, he will give money away, he will never bother looking at price tags, he'll have a thin red car and a big vicious dog and he'll spend his holidays at the snow. His fabulous two-storey house will have an in-ground pool and a colour television with pushbuttons and a matching pair of leather recliner chairs and a dishwasher and a chest freezer and a tropical fish tank and an outdoor spa and a spiral staircase and a separate bedroom for every person who lives there . . . a house not much unlike the Jensons', he supposes. He has wondered, on Colt's and Bastian's behalf, what they could possibly be getting for Christmas, and has decided it will probably be a trampoline. They seem to like toys they can share. Either a trampoline or a Green Machine, to add to their collection of fantastic wheeled playthings.

He doesn't know how he'll earn the money to sustain his anticipated life of luxury. He won't be a printer, like his father—printing's brought him nothing so far. Sometimes—and Syd does not tell Declan this—he thinks about a life of crime. It sounds exciting and, if one can stay out of gaol, seems a flash way to earn a living. A cat-burglar. A bank robber. He pictures himself wielding a gun. He could ask Garrick about that kind of thing, but Garrick would only big-note himself, though he's never done anything more impressive than filch some lollies from the milkbar. Syd Kiley the gangster, thinks Syd Kiley the boy, will laugh in the face of Garrick Greene, then squash him like an ant.

But this lies a long way in the future: for now, skateboards are his concern, and he hasn't got any money so he must pin his hopes on Santa Claus, in whom he has some faith but not belief. He doesn't need an extravagant board, just something with a bit of dash, preferably one with red-and-white chevrons like Colt's board, although in truth almost any kind will do. His friends will expect not only to hear about it, but to see it and ride it: so if he doesn't get it, he might as well die. He'd be better off. He lies listening to the murmur of his parents' voices, and in a lightning-bolt instant he is decided. Living in hope is simply too precarious, he must take matters into his own hands. It's always best to ask their father for something — money, that's all the children really want — when he is sober. When he's been drinking, he is both miserly and impoverished. He will undoubtedly say no, but at least the thought will be put in his head; more importantly, his mother will witness the depth of his desire, the risks he's prepared to take for it. It's a brave move, to get out of bed, interrupt their conversation, request a costly something. It's likely that what he'll get for his trouble is more trouble — a shout to get to his bedroom, a whack to hurry him along. But once the decision is made, he can't resist.

He slips from bed and out the door quickly, and pads down the hall on bare feet, the cuffs of his pyjamas flipping at his ankles. The kitchen light is on but he veers around the patch of fluorescence it casts into the hall. He hesitates in the shadows of the lounge doorway, collecting his meagre courage. From here he can't see his parents but they are there, very near, and very far away. The television is on, not loudly. He hears his mother say something about school fees, and his father replies, "Yes, I suppose." His tone is testy, and Syd's nerve wavers. He could go back to bed and his parents would never know he'd stood here in secret, overhearing them. But his mind is essentially the one-track kind, and this plan is all he has. He's on the verge of stepping from the shadows and into the room when his mother says, "Syd and Declan said something funny about Rex Jenson today."

Syd instantly ducks back into the darkness. "Who's Rex Jenson," says his father.

"Oh, you know. The man who cooked the barbeque the other day. The people with the pool."

"The dentist? He's a try-hard, that bloke."

"Well. Him."

The TV burbles and Syd's father must listen; after a minute he asks, "What about him."

"The boys were saying . . ." Syd can tell his mother is at the ironing-board, because she pauses the way she does when she's turning a garment to press its intimate spots. "They were saying he rubs their shoulders, that sort of thing. Declan told Syd not to go to their house by himself."

There's quite a long lull in which neither Syd's mother nor father speaks. Laughter erupts from the television, there's a bad-tempered sigh from the iron. The audience applauds, and the TV show cuts to an ad: still his parents say nothing. Then his father says, "We had teachers like that when I was at school. *Over-friendly.*"

"Maybe you should say something to him."

"To who? The dentist?"

"Obviously, Joe."

Again they are silent, and the advertisements jangle. Syd rests his head against the doorframe, feels the severe bite of the wood. Eventually his father speaks. "If it's just a rub on the shoulders, there's not much harm done. Is there."

"I don't know. Is there?"

"It never hurt us. We used to laugh it off."

"That's what they're doing, I think, laughing it off."

"Well, good." Joe shifts on the couch and the vinyl cushions creak. "You have to feel sorry for blokes like that," he says. "They're pathetic." Again the adults are silent, and the television noise expands. The program they are watching resumes with a fanfare, and Syd hears his father guffaw. The host of the show talks in a pompous way, his voice like rough-sawn timber. It's mortally boring, this program, although grownups find it hilarious. Then Joe says, "I don't know what you expect me to do. We've got to live with these people, they're only up the road. I'm not gonna march up there and make a hoo-ha over nothing."

"Declan wouldn't have mentioned it, if it was nothing—"

"Well, tell him to toughen up. There's nothing worse than a crybaby. Nothing worse than a dobber, either."

"He wasn't dobbing," says Elizabeth. "Oh, forget it," she says.

And his father does go quiet, so Syd thinks he might be forgetting it. But then he chuckles and says, "God Almighty. Poor bloody bloke. He's a bit of a dickhead, I agree, but that doesn't mean he should be stoned in the square."

"Don't carry on, Joe. I'm only telling you."

"We don't even know if it's true, do we? The boys could have it all wrong. They probably do, knowing them. You want me to make a fool of myself, bang on his door and accuse the poor sod of something that never happened?"

Syd doesn't hear what his mother replies; he moves away from the door and down the hall as if drawn by the arms of a ghost. He doesn't want to ask his father for anything anymore. His chest feels filled with oil, a contempt that takes the shape of a hooded snake racing through burning grass. He climbs into bed and draws up the blankets, lies staring into the dark. He thinks one word, a favourite of his, thinks it repeatedly as the baleful snake rips across the flames. Chickenshit, he thinks: you *chickenshit.*

It's a word Freya hears him whisper when, a couple of nights later, they are gathered at the window staring wide-eyed through the darkness to where their father is kicking the flanks of Elizabeth's car. The station wagon absorbs each wallop with a stolid thunk. Marigold is sobbing, her fingers dragging at her cheeks, and Peter in his mother's arms is crying uncertainly, but the rest of them are silent, watching the performance and waiting for what comes next, until Freya hears Syd say, "Chickenshit," and she glances at him, and his face is steeped with rage.

All the lights inside the house are off, as is the veranda light. A blackout might have deterred their father, but all it is doing is throwing a gauzy cloak over his rampage. He moves unsteadily around the car, lashing unpredictably at the plants along the fence, kicking the car in every panel, growling as he goes. He's a jerking, jolting shape in the night, there's nothing liquid about him. The station wagon is as solid as a tank, imperturbable: booting it makes their father stumble, arms thrust out rigidly. Then he lurches forward, swings his leg again, and a door takes the impact with a boom. Marigold, at Freya's elbow, covers her ears and weeps.

And it might be that he knows they're watching, for he goes still, all of a sudden, and turns to the house, his feet shuffling to keep him upright; he turns a full circle before dropping to a crouch by the front passenger wheel. Freya asks huskily, "What's he doing?" and in the next instant she knows. The corner of the car doesn't drop significantly, but the moonlight shifts on the bonnet. Then Joe crabwalks down the side of the car to the next tyre, and as he lets the air out of this too, the list of the vehicle becomes obvious. Two sunken tyres might be enough, but he seems committed to the work now, and scuttles around to the far side of the car. Freya shades her eyes against the window, scanning what she can see of the street. It's late, not far from midnight, yet surely someone will notice a madman in a front garden and telephone the police. Surely somebody must hear their hearts. Rescue has never come when they've needed it, but Freya can't bring herself to accept that they are alone in this. The world seems to abandon them to their plight at such times, but it shouldn't—it has no right to. It cannot ignore them, and expect them to forgive that, and forget it—to emerge from neglect unscathed. They have, she thinks, such reason to be resentful.

Her siblings have, anyway.

When all four tyres are flat as puddles their father rises up to lean against the bonnet, wiping his palms on his chest. The sight of him spills fresh tears from Marigold, and their mother reaches to her. "It's all right," she says: but what is all right about a woman and a clutch of petrified children standing in an unlit lounge room watching a man deflate the tyres of their car so they won't use the vehicle to escape him — what is all right about that? If she and Declan were older, Freya thinks, they could go out there and knock him down, beat him with something heavy on the back of the head, but she's not capable of doing it yet, and it will be a long time until she is — a long time of standing here, gripping Dorrie's wrist, sinking in this stew of fright and guilt.

He turns to the window, where he must know they are, and shouts, "Let me in!"

That is the cause: the screen door is locked, and he doesn't have a key. It's so late, and Elizabeth had thought he wasn't coming home, or maybe that he didn't deserve to, so she'd locked the door before going to bed. And now he is sagging, drained, against the bonnet, having kicked the screen door violently and so noisily before attacking the car, and Freya crosses her fingers hoping he'll drop dead with exhaustion — or not dead, just unconscious, for she doesn't hate her father, she loves him — but what she's terrified will really happen is that he'll hurl a brick through a window, take an axe to the door, rummage in the garage for petrol and set the house alight. They are standing at the window because here are the glass doors through which they can run if they need to, across the garden, over the street, into the parkland and the night. She will clamp her hand round Dorrie's paw and drag her if she has to, running like a gazelle.

"Let me in!" he screams, and slams a fist against the bonnet making the loudest noise ever heard in this neighbourhood, a sonic blast which crumples Marigold to the floor. In her mind's eye Freya sees the house burn, the car explode, the pine tree in the yard become a whooshing candle of flame. If this is the future then they have to let him in. And there's a confused part of her that might have carried her to the door and unlocked it, some pious piece which solemnly believes that she, Freya, must take what's coming—except that her father abruptly pushes away from the car and shambles not toward the house or garage but to where his own car is parked messily on the driveway, its driver's door hanging open. They watch him climb behind the wheel and there's a drawn-out, soundless minute that is almost suffocating—in his car could be a screwdriver, a crowbar, even, she thinks, a gun—and Dorrie whimpers, "What's he doing?" and Declan hisses, "Shh!"

Then their father's car roars and the headlamps glare into wakefulness, spearing beams across the lawn. Oh no, Freya thinks: no no no no. He is going to ram the house. She wants to scream at her family to get back from the window, for the glass when it shatters will be like flying scimitars, the car will surge smoking and screeching into the room, the walls and ceiling will crash down to seal them in a splintery, fume-filled tomb. But none of these words come out of her, because it's hopeless to flee. The world has been pulled off-kilter, and something horrendous is now running on the loose. Its quarry is she, Freya Kiley. In its fury it has possessed her father and is shaking him to pieces, but it's Freya whom it really wants. She thinks to tell her family, *You'll be safe, I will go:* but then her father's car rams backwards into the street, comes to a jarring halt as the gears change, and drives, dark as a tumour, away.

For some time they linger near the window, expecting him to return, although the neighbourhood is quiet enough for them to hear his car burling further and further away. Marigold mops her face and gets up from the floor, and Dorrie rubs her squeezed wrist. When, after a while, he hasn't returned, Elizabeth tells her children to go to bed. It's a school night, it is late. Freya lies feeling her body float past the ceiling and into the empty sky. Tonight she's seen the front door bludgeoned from its hinges with an axe, the roof of her house fringed with fire, the trees in the garden swathed in flame, knives of glass twirling around her. She's seen herself running, running for her actual life, hauling her sister over concrete and road. She's seen, after all these years, the wraith-like creature that has been thinking about her forever, crouched golden-eyed in the darkness, waiting for its chance. And all there is to show for it are four flat tyres and a few scuff-marks on a car: who, she wonders dully, would believe it.

Rex: she sits across from him and drinks tea that Tabby has made, and as she talks Freya detects no doubt in his eyes, nothing to show he isn't taking what she says with the utmost seriousness. She's here because she had to come, the need to speak to him had been a weight like stones on her ribs. He'd been outside watering the garden as he often does after dinner, but it seemed like he was waiting for her. As she'd approached the house she remembered Declan telling Syd not to go there alone: but Declan should get on his knees and beg to be forgiven. "Good evening," Rex had said, gathering the hose in loops. "Would you like a cup of tea?"

So she's sitting on the deck opposite him, her gaze on the spangling surface of the pool, telling him about the beaten station wagon and how, the next morning, their father made no apology: how he'd had, as he always had, nothing to say about the night before, as if he didn't remember or it had never happened or it had nothing to do with him. He'd cooked pikelets for his children's breakfast, and as she'd eaten at the kitchen table Freya had studied him when she had the chance. Joe has never seemed particularly interested in her. He lets her help tinker with the cars, but he doesn't need her; he doesn't talk to her about the jazz records he buys or what he did when he was a boy, he's never told her he is a good dancer. If they had a cat, she muses, an animal that ate and slept and crossed one's path unnecessarily, that cat could be what she is to Joe. Yet for her, because of her, he endures this sour life: going off each morning to the printery, coming home each night to a family he's allowed to drift into dreading him, a life of blotted bruises and forgotten hours and empty pockets, and years of the same ahead. It's a life run into a ditch—and her mother's life is too, the realisation that she didn't need a husband or children having come too late to save her. The things they don't want are all they have.

A leaf has blown onto the surface of the pool, and the breeze spins it like a pixie's raft caught in a whirlpool. Bastian is rambling on hands and knees among the trees, pushing a metal dumptruck as large as a loaf of bread. His mother has gone into the garden with him, strolling along clearing the truck's path with her foot as she goes. And Colt, who is wearing his school trousers and shirt with the sleeves rolled up and the tail of the shirt untucked, is sitting on the steps listening as his father listens, soberly and without comment. His hair has fallen forward, there are notes written in biro on his brown forearm. She can't decide if she'd prefer him to go. It is, despite everything, another beautiful night. "I wish they would leave each other," she says. "I wish Mum would make him leave."

Rex says, "Some things are more complicated than you imagine."

"She should try harder—"

"It's not your mother's fault, Freya. Don't blame her."

She shuts her mouth, reproof tingling her face. Bastian guffaws as the truck topples head-over-wheels down the BMX ramp. From one of the trees a blackbird lets loose its call, having spotted the neighbour's black-and-white cat dodging along the top rail of the fence. Colt says, "Puss," and twitches his fingers, but the cat only stares ponderously at him before moving on.

"I know whose fault it is," Freya says. "It's mine."

Rex lifts a brow. "Why do you think that?"

"Well." She stops, it is so awkward. "Remember you said they might have got married for babies? Well, they did. I was the baby. I found out what day they got married, and I worked it out."

"I see." He's as calm as a river. She looks at his hands closed loosely around his mug, and thinks of those hands in flesh-coloured gloves, cradling aching jaws. The drill-sound of unhappiness always in his ears. He sees, yet she feels compelled to explain, "If I hadn't been born, they wouldn't have got married, and none of what happens would happen. So it's my fault, isn't it."

Rex smiles as he must smile at nervous children in the chair: as if they're silly for imagining he'd even know how to hurt them. "That's a foolish thing to say," he tells her. "You know it is, so I won't indulge it. None of us are responsible for the circumstances of our birth."

She stares into her cup, disgraced, but mulishly determined. Breathing deeply, she looks up to meet his eye. "Even if it's foolish, it's still a fact. They wouldn't have got married if not for me. And that makes me . . . guilty."

Colt has rested his forehead on his folded arms. His hair catches the setting sun and shines like hot copper. Tabby and Bastian are walking the perimeter of the pool, Bastian in the lead, Tabby pretending she's secretly plotting to capture him; he squeaks and scurries when she gets too close, then lets her catch up again. The neighbour's cat has settled on a fencepost and with a droll eye is watching their game. Freya hesitates, but finally says what she's come to say. "I've been thinking about something strange. It's dumb, but I can't stop thinking it. The other night, when I thought Dad was going to smash the house with his car, I imagined this creature—this *monster* that's black and slinky, like a big black lion, with long shiny claws and yellow eyes. It runs really fast, and it has fangs like a shark. And it wants me. It's been coming for me since I was born, because I wasn't supposed to be—born, I mean. Me being born . . . messed things up. Other things should have happened, but they couldn't, because of me. So the monster's chasing me, not to make things different because it's too late now . . . but because someone has to pay for things being messed around. And since I'm the one who did it, it's me it wants, and when it gets me things will still be wrong but they'll be less wrong, because I'll have been . . ."

"Sacrificed?" says Rex.

She looks up from the table. "Yeah. I think so. I won't die or disappear or anything like that. But I'm meant to be unhappy. It wants me to be unhappy, to even out how unhappy Dad is, and Mum is. And that seems . . . fair."

Rex contemplates her, his eyes moving over her cheeks, chin

and mouth. He doesn't reach for her hand as she'd like him to, or even smile at her. "Freya," he says. "Do you think it's what your father and mother want — for you to be unhappy?"

"No," she admits. "But the monster doesn't care."

"There is no monster. There's no such thing. There's no such thing as the way things were *supposed* to be. And you are not responsible for how other people live their lives — you know that, don't you?"

"Yes," she says, although she doesn't know, not honestly. She says, "I know the monster isn't real. If it was real I couldn't hide from it, not even for a day. It would see me. It would see me when I was asleep. It would see inside my head and hear what I was thinking."

"Like God," says Colt into his arms.

Rex glances at his son and smiles; Freya likes it, how he's a father who smiles. Joe, she realises, never smiles. He looks at her and says, still smiling, "For what it's worth, I'm glad you were born. I'm glad your brothers and sisters were born. If you messed things up, Freya Kiley, I think you messed them up the right way."

She grins at the tabletop shyly. She could wish her own father were more like him — generous with affection and wisdom — but she won't, not if it means having Rex become less special, cool the warm cradle that is his attention. If she has to choose, she chooses Rex. "OK," she says: and goes home feeling strong, as if she's been suited in armour.

Syd and Declan ride their bikes to the stormwater drain. The school holidays are nearing, and the promise of them seems to tense and sparkle the air. Syd is not a child for sleeping-in or mooching around home, and he has plans for the holidays. He will ride to some point further than he's ever been. He will construct a habitat for camping outside overnight. He will explore the drain, having added a torch to his wishlist. And he will master the skateboard which he craves so hungrily now that surely the world must fit itself around him, he can't possibly be denied. "What do you want for Christmas?" he shouts to his brother, who is speeding down the road's centre beside him, and Declan shakes his whipping hair and says, "I dunno! I don't care!" And that is incredible to Syd, that someone should have the chance to receive something for nothing and yet be utterly lacking in greed and grandiosity. Syd will never be like Declan, his brother will forever be a mystery to him: but if he thinks about life without him, Syd sees himself flying off the way screwed-up paper skitters over a table when a door opens and a gale comes in.

Apart from a woman walking a dog far across the grass, the wasteland is as deserted as always. The creek into which the stormwater flows is stinky with the morning's warmth, a sweaty, mouldering smell. Along the bank, in every nook of rock and earth, are jumbles of leaves and twigs and rubbish that have been catching in these corners for years. The crusty piles are solid with sludge and time, and don't budge when Syd kicks them. He likes to inspect the drifts regularly, for the creek is eternally adding to them. Avery claims to have once found a five-dollar note planted like a pink flag in one of the drifts. Syd would be satisfied with cash, but he fantasises about finding a limb. He would like a foot in a shoe or an arm with a tattoo. He would like an entire body, but would not, he thinks, care for just a head.

The smell of the creek reaches them before they see its glinting water, and as they swing onto the track that weaves through the grassland Syd is riding fast, standing on his pedals, his bike jinking and squeaking under him. The wind on his face is so pleasant that he yelps with the joy of being alive. Summer is here, the season that is the great friend of boys; this year he will amass a collection of cicada shells to rival all previous collections combined. It is a perfect morning for two brothers to be powering their trusty bikes down a stone track with most of the weekend ahead of them and no one around to bother them, and summer is here, and Christmas is coming, and school is as good as done.

Declan hits his brakes and the rear tyre of his bike cuts a fanning groove in the path; Syd pulls up behind him saying, "What?"

They are within sight of the cavernous mouth of the drain,

and dumped among the weeds on the bank is a bicycle. "That's Garrick's bike," says Declan.

At once Syd's happiness deflates. "Let's keep going, Deco."

But his brother skims his bike closer to where Garrick's bike lies, leans over his handlebars to get a better view down the bank to the pipe. "Garrick?" he calls. "Are you in there?"

There is no immediate answer; then a stone whizzes out from the mouth of the tunnel and lands with a brown splash in the water. The Kileys look back to the drain. "Garrick?" says Declan.

The bulky boy's voice comes from the pipe's shadows like the voice of a dragon from a cave. "Wadda you want?"

". . . Nothing. We saw your bike."

There's a pause in which Syd squints against the sun and sky, wishing he could sprout wings and flap away. On the opposite bank a paper bag, blown up like a balloon, is bopping and gusting its leisurely way across the land. "Who's with you?" Garrick demands, and Syd sighs.

"It's just me and Syd—"

"Not that Jenson homo?"

"No, just me and Syd."

Immediately Garrick materialises at the mouth of the drain—he must have been closer than Syd realised. For all his talk, he is scared to go deep into the tunnel. Having ascertained that the bike is safe and that Garrick Greene is not only alive but also in a foul mood, Syd sees no reason why he and Declan should not resume their carefree cruise; but Declan has kicked down the stand of his bike and is stepping from rock to reliable rock down the embankment to the water, and Syd has no choice but to follow. One day, he vows silently, he will make Garrick pay.

Inside the pipe the air is cool as it always is, with the same decomposing smell, like the air inside a haunted house. Garrick has retreated to slouch against the pipe's wall, the worn toes of his runners taking his weight. He looks squeezed into his striped t-shirt. His face has been chipped from granite. "What are you doing?" Declan asks, and Garrick says, "What does it look like?" It looks like a lot of things, so Declan doesn't say anything. The boys linger beneath the cresting concrete, waiting for something to change. Then, "Look," says Garrick, and takes from his pocket the cap of a softdrink bottle. In its shallow basin are microscopic letters: *You have won a portable radio!* Declan quirks an eyebrow. "Where'd you get that?"

"Sister got it. Said I could have it."

Syd doesn't ask if the sister in question is the one with the baby or the one who ran away or the one whose underwear Garrick steals: frankly, he's not interested. And he knows that if he had such a bottlecap Garrick would deride it, saying they give away a thousand radios and how they're the kind which nobody wants and that there's always a catch with such prizes so he'll probably find when he goes to collect it that he's actually won a sun visor or a free game at a bowling alley, all this poison hucked out because nothing good's allowed to happen to anyone . . . so Syd's startled when Garrick sends the bottlecap soaring through the air, out the pipe and into the water where it bobs frantically for an instant before being swallowed from sight. "Shit," says Garrick.

Declan looks away from the place where the cap disappeared; Syd can see him struggling to work out what's going on. Garrick is not typically a complex man. "Could have given it to me," Declan says carefully.

Garrick sneers. "What would you do with a portable radio? Listen to cricket in the shed like some codger?"

"Maybe." Declan doesn't point out that Garrick himself likes cricket. "I would have tied it to the handlebars."

Garrick thinks about this—the notion of having a radio attached to one's bike, of being able to play music or follow sport while also riding around—and Syd sees, with some relish, that he's kicking himself. "Too late now," he says. "Should have said before."

And then he does, in fact, kick something—he spins and boots the concrete wall even as the slope of the pipe sends him sliding into the slime. It's a hard kick, and must hurt, for he's wearing just old canvas runners, but he doesn't wince: if he'll never be anything else, Garrick is undeniably tough. He prides himself on being a boy of steel—yet here he is, kicking the wall. And Syd feels a pinprick of disquiet.

The slime is a staining substance, and it smudges Garrick's white shoes. He lifts a foot out of the gunk and shakes it. "Ah, shit," he says. "Shit!"

To Syd's vast relief, Declan finally sees sense. "We better go," he says.

"Yeah, piss off!"

". . . You can come with us, if you want. Look for taddies or something."

"No, piss off, cockwipes! Get lost! Go play your baby games by yourselves."

Declan regards him. "OK," he says. "Come on, Syd."

The brothers pick their way up the embankment, Syd fighting the urge to run, but they're not at the top when Garrick reappears at the pipe's mouth. "Hey," he says. "We gotta do something about that perv."

Declan pauses and straightens, looking back. Syd stops behind him, trapped on the narrow climbing route on both sides of which the weeds grow chest-high, studded with barbs and insects. "What do you mean?"

"You know." Garrick gazes at them leadenly. "You know who I mean. Avery said you were all laughing about it. What's so funny about a perv, Deco? Like pervs, do you?"

Syd feels an almost frenzied desire not to become embroiled in what can only be a miserable conversation: but Declan, standing with the weeds shushing round him, asks, "What's happened?"

"Nothing funny, that's for sure." But instead of telling them anything, Garrick's mouth warps and his hefty hands wag. "I'm not yelling it out for the whole world to hear."

"Let's go," Syd whispers, so softly it is scarcely more than a thought, and Declan only glances at him; Syd follows him unhappily back down the slope to the drain. Garrick has edged into the shadows, but the brothers stop at the entrance of the pipe so the sun stays on their shoulders and they could run if they had to, through the water and up the far bank, into the obscurity of the scrub.

But now they are here again, Garrick's suddenly offhand. He kicks the pipe, tosses his fringe, hawks up a gob of spit. He peers down the tunnel as if he's heard his name called. Without looking at them he says, "He wasn't naked," and adds swiftly, "Neither was I. He didn't make me touch his toggle—"

Syd, to whom the idea of touching someone else's toggle is completely new and even more completely horrifying, makes a rodent's noise, and Garrick wheels, glaring. "Tell him to wait with the bikes, Deco!"

"No, Syd should know." Declan darts a frown at his brother. "Keep quiet. So what happened?"

Garrick grunts, and settles awkwardly against the pipe, his knee a battering-ram in front of him. He seems to chew on his words before letting them out. "Me and Avery were there having a swim last night. You know why he put that pool in, don't you? He was sitting on the deck, the way he does. Making his stupid comments. Anyway, it was getting late, dinnertime, so Avery said we had to go. We had our towels hanging on a tree, not up on the deck. So we get out of the pool and get dressed fast, just pulling on our clothes over our bathers. And he's watching like he does, he comes down as if he's got something to do in the garden, he comes down and he's standing there, pretending he's looking at something in the grass. And then, as we go past, he goes, *What an untidy pair you are*—you know the homo way he speaks—*take pride in your appearance, boys.* And he doesn't get Avery because that slippery bastard jumped out of the way: but he grabs me and, really quick, he tucks my shirt into my jeans. He sticks his fingers down the back of my jeans, stuffing my shirt in." Garrick's voice has become wobbly and heated, and when he looks at his friends there is craziness in his eyes. "He cops a feel of my arse, Declan!"

Declan, hands on head, says, "Yeah. That's shit."

"Yeah it's shit!" Garrick's voice slams down the tunnel. "Touching my arse!"

"Where was Colt?"

"How would I know? He was there, and then he wasn't there. I don't know where he went. He should have been there. It wouldn't have happened if he'd been there—"

"It's not Colt's fault—"

"Nah?" Garrick gulps, eyes bulging. "It's his dad, isn't it? Not my dad or your dad: *his* dad."

Declan's hands drop. "What happened then?"

"What? I went home—"

"Did you say anything to him?"

"No! What was I gonna say? *Enjoy that, perv?* But he was lucky that when I went home my brothers weren't there. When I tell them, they're gonna stuff his bloody hands down his throat!"

"Don't tell them," says Declan.

Both Garrick and Syd look at him, surprised. "What?" says Garrick. "Why not?"

"Because . . ." Declan pauses, wincing. "Because it's not that bad, is it? It's not. But if your brothers stuff his hands down his throat, it *will* be bad."

Garrick stares, incredulous. Then, "Not that bad!" he bellows, and his voice, in the pipe, is ear-splitting. “He touched my arse, Declan! My *arse*!”

Declan nods and nods. “Yeah, I heard you. But what’s the point of making a big deal about it? You can’t do anything. You can’t prove it.”

Garrick squeals, “Bloody hell! You reckon I should forget it? Let him touch my arse and *forget it*? What’s wrong with you? You like that sort of stuff, do you? You reckon it’s OK?”

“No—”

“You do! You like it! You’re a bloody perv too! You’re as disgusting as he is!”

Declan’s lip curls, and his blue eyes go flinty. The sunshine haloes his edges as he stands cool and still and dignified. “All right,” he says calmly, “tell your brothers. Tell them how you let a man touch your prick. You know what he’s like, you knew he was gonna do it, and you stood there and let him. See what they say about that.”

Garrick stares black murder. “You shithead. That’s not how it was, and you know it. I should kill you for saying that.”

“It’s not me saying it,” Declan replies. “It’s what everyone else will say.”

Garrick’s nostrils flare as he absorbs this, he swallows what sounds like a brick. “He didn’t touch my prick,” he says finally. “He touched my arse, I told you.”

“And did it set your arse on fire?” Syd is speaking before he knows words are coming out: Declan and Garrick turn to him in astonishment as he plunges delinquently on. “Don’t be a crybaby,

Garrick. We don't like that man either, but being a crybaby and a dobber is worse. If you make a big fuss we'll never get to swim in the pool or ride the BMX or play with the slot cars or anything ever again, get it?"

Garrick stares, his eyes jumping over Syd's face. Death-coldly he says, "The only reason I'm not punching your head in right now, you shit, is because I've got more important things to think about, get it? I don't care about *toys.* I'm not a baby."

Syd quavers, but he does not budge. Never in his life has he been as bold as he wants to be: never, until this minute. He says, "My dad was kicking my mum's car the other night. He was yelling, swearing, calling us names. He comes home drunk and he punches the walls, he slams doors, he's smashed all Mum's favourite things. My sisters cry because they're frightened, they hide under their beds. One time he pulled my mum's hair, and he pulled out such a chunk that her head was bleeding. He gives her Chinese burns, and he spits on her. When we hear his car come home, we feel sick, wondering what's going to happen—if he's going to fall asleep telling some story, or if he's gonna kick the cupboards in, or throw a glass at Mum, or hold his fist in Declan's face and tell him to get to bed. But no one cares about any of that, do they? No one says he should have his hands stuffed down his throat."

He stops as cleanly as if he's run into a ditch. Declan has long looked away. They know that Garrick's father is a hard man, and that the boy will understand—will know the sound of a door swinging with force into a wall. "It's not the same," says Garrick, but weakly, and Syd barks like a fox, "It's worse, isn't it? But I don't see your tough brothers doing anything about it."

"Leave my brothers out of this—"

"I will if you will."

Garrick snorts, smiles darkly. He scrapes the sole of his runner down the pipe, making a coarse crumbling sound. In the quiet that follows they hear water dripping deep inside the drain. Garrick wipes his nose and looks at the brothers. "You must both be homos," he says. "Your dad and that man—it's not the same."

"It's not the same," Declan agrees, "but it's just—life, isn't it? So just live with it. Just stay out of his way—"

"Oh, I'm going to! He's not getting his hands on me again—"

"Well, good."

"—but this shit has to be paid for, Declan. I don't care what you say. He can't just get away with it—that's not right. It's just not right!"

Declan nods slowly. "What about Colt?"

"What about him? What about him? It's his bloody dad. He should have been there—if he'd been there, it wouldn't have happened!"

The boys size each other up: none of them will budge, and it is pointless to argue further. "What are you going to do?" Declan asks, and Garrick snaps, "I dunno. Something." Silence follows, and the situation settles snowily around them, cold and bright-white. Garrick picks up a pebble, examines it, and pings it with accuracy at Syd. It hits the boy's elbow and zings away. "Call me a crybaby again," he says, "and I will break your arm. Got it?"

Syd, clutching his arm, doesn't answer. "*Got it*?" says Garrick.

"Yeah," says Syd.

Declan steps to the brink of the pipe and stands gazing over the water with his hands in his pockets and the morning sunshine lacquering his cheeks. The paper bag which is like a balloon has rolled and bumped its way a fair distance downstream. "I've got money," Garrick says eventually. "Let's go to the milkbar."

Colt sits astride his racer, watching Avery teach Bastian to ride a skateboard. Both boys are light-footed, but Avery, the street cat, places his feet exactly where they're needed, while Bastian — his poor brother who'd have been better off being born a girl or maybe a canary, something pretty and safe in a cage — is as awkward as a baby giraffe. Colt watches him trundle along the road, pips of bitumen almost shaking him from the board, each tentative paddle of his toes against the ground eliciting a nervy grimace. Avery says, "Don't stand in the middle of the board, Bas!" and Bastian, as is his way, shouts, "I know, I know how to do it!" and moves his foot from the centre to the very end of the board: and the skateboard's nose lifts like a sniffing dog's snout and swings violently toward its master's ankle. The boy jumps clear, hands flailing, and the board starts to escape downhill. Bastian looks back helplessly: "Go and get it!" Colt urges, and the child gallops away. Colt's gaze follows him, and he wonders where on earth his brother will go.

Avery perches on the gutter, the red-and-white board across his thighs. Its chunky wheels are flecked with small dents from the road. Colt props his wrists on the racer's handlebars. "I thought you didn't have a skateboard."

"I don't."

"So how did you learn to ride?"

Avery shrugs. "Sometimes you just know what to do, I guess."

Colt thinks of how he used to run, his body knowing how to do it without wondering how it knew, his coach often telling him that he had great natural style, relaxed but controlled, that he ran the way a javelin flew, with no energy wasted. Lately he's begun to yearn for that feeling again — not just the fast feel of the track under his toes, but the certainty that, lining up against a rival, he will win. In general he hates to see others fail or be hurt, yet on the track he had known a kind of mercilessness. He'd had no friends, no brother, nothing to which he was obliged. He looks away from that past — he'll never run a track again, never crouch, with beatless heart, before the gun, never look into the stands to see his father there, knuckly hands between his knees — but maybe he can run these hilly streets alone. He feels that solitude will suit him. He looks down at Avery, at the knee which is patched with a scab like a swatch of buffalo leather. The wound must be itching as it heals, because occasionally Avery rubs it with a palm. He is wearing a t-shirt that has a long split in the seam, and Colt has the peculiar thought that he could give everything he owns to Avery Price — toys, clothes, books, bed, pool, the racers and the BMX, the footballs and the tennis racquets, the school uniform and the school and the excellent report cards and the home-cooked meals, the ribbons and the trophies, the mother and father and brother—and take off running. Unburdened, he would achieve a speed that would first blur him and then stretch him into fine wire-lines of colour which would spool out into invisibility.

Bastian hasn't returned, and Colt lifts his head. His brother is halfway down the street, in the middle of the road, the skateboard cradled to his chest, staring down the hill to where Declan, Syd and Garrick have appeared on their bikes. They are moving up the road slowly, the older boys slightly ahead of the younger one. They have seen Colt and Avery and Bastian, had seen them before being seen. In the gutter Avery straightens, and Colt adjusts his hold on the handlebars. He tells himself there's nothing particular to fear—nothing he doesn't know already, nothing changed from how it was five minutes or even five seconds ago—yet his blood has started to surge. He would call Bastian to him but some instinct tells him that not only would this be summoning his brother to a place of greater danger, but that the child's slightest movement will set the approaching boys running like wolves. So the three of them remain where they are—Avery in the gutter, Colt astride his bike, Bastian marooned in the sunny centre of the road—as their friends cruise uphill, and it's only when they are near enough for Colt to read the fraying stickers on the frame of Garrick's bike that they stop, Syd hanging back, lurking in shadows that aren't there. Garrick's face shows nothing, he doesn't even look at Colt. He frowns at Avery and says, "Get up. Grab your bike."

Avery is not one to be ordered about. "Why?"

"We're going to the shop, that's why. You're coming with us."

". . . What about Colt and Bastian?"

"What about Colt and Bastian?" Garrick sing-songs. "I'm not talking to them, am I? I'm talking to you. And I'm telling you to get your bike and come with us. You're not staying here with the perv. He can stick his hands down his own pants today." Then he swings his heavy head to Colt, and Colt sees in his face the razor-cuts of his rage. "You and your brother stay here, so daddy can play with *his boys.*"

Colt glances from Garrick to Declan, who is staring at his bike's shell-less bell. The sun becomes a sudden inferno, claws tigerishly at the nape of Colt's neck. He looks downhill to his brother and sees the boy is watching him, his angel-face furrowed, on the verge of saying something which doesn't need to be said. "You should go," Colt tells Avery.

Declan doesn't look up from the exposed innards of the bell when he says, "Yeah. Come on, Avery."

And Avery the street cat decides that at this moment in these circumstances the smart thing to do is to put the skateboard aside and hoist his bike up from the naturestrip, and, with his eyes low and in a voice like something blown along a lane, say, "See you later, Colt."

"No you won't," says Garrick. "You're never seeing him again. You're our friend, not his." And turning his glare on Colt he says, "You prick. You shouldn't have come here. You should have stayed in the shitheap where you belong."

He shoves past Colt, driving down on his pedals so his bike heaves away; Avery follows him, swooping widely over the road. Colt watches them go, the world draining speedily through his fingers: he turns to Declan and says, "It's not our fault—"

"Yeah, I know." Declan spins the pedal into place beneath his foot. "But . . . you know."

He pushes the bike forward, passing Colt without looking at him; and only then remembers his brother, and looks back. Syd stands with his feet planted either side of his bike, mouth set, cheeks ashen. At Declan he shouts defiantly, "I don't do what *Garrick* says!"

Declan circles his bike once, twice. "Do what *I* say," he says. "Get going."

He swings the bicycle and powers after his friends; Syd tears air between his teeth and it is a sob of grief and fury. "Fuck!" he says, and shoves his bike into motion. Avery and Garrick have already disappeared around the corner; Syd catches his brother and in moments they too round the corner, out of sight.

The street becomes soundless again. The sun blazes brilliantly off cars and the footpath. Bastian comes cautiously closer, hugging the skateboard, his sights fixed on the point where the neighbourhood boys had last been. When they don't reappear, he looks at Colt. "What's happening?" he asks. "Why is everyone swearing?"

And Colt can't make himself say anything, feeling it even as he stands there, held upright only by strings: the smearing of his outline, the thinning of his colours, and it isn't because he is flying like a javelin—he's never felt heavier, more summoned to the ground—but because something has gripped him and is peeling him into nothing, some sleek, clawed, yellow-eyed hunting thing which can hear the very thoughts in his head.

On Sunday Freya tells her mother, "No, I'm not going."

Elizabeth looks as if her firstborn child has removed a mask which Elizabeth never guessed she'd been wearing: "Yes you are," she says, but Freya replies, "No I'm not, so don't tell me again. What's God ever done for me?"

Elizabeth's gaze hardens. "You sound like your father."

"Why shouldn't I?" Freya laughs. The heart is wicked. "He's my father. You chose him."

Dorrie and Marigold stand goggling, struck by the possibilities that have opened up before their eyes. "I'm not going either!" Marigold pipes.

"You are!" says Elizabeth, and swats her; before marching away she throws Freya a look meant to cut her in two. It only makes Freya feel more certain. In the last few days there's been nothing that hasn't made her feel this way—each dog's bark and crust of bread and twinge of discomfort and hair fallen in her eyes, every sight she's seen and sound she's heard has felt like the imparting of a piece of vital information. She is travelling toward something and although she has no idea what it is she knows in her bones that her path is true. Refusing to go to church would, just weeks ago, have been an act of towering courage: now she's done it casually, and certainly without apology. If she has spent her life rummaging through a castle of countless rooms, she thinks she must have found the vault at the castle's core, because inside it there is nothing but her wits. She has pushed aside Heaven and armed herself with reason, and now she is making a stand. She wants to disappoint her mother, because when the moment comes—and she doesn't know when that will be, but it will be soon, for the wait is never long, the days follow each other in a kind of lurching clockwork—she wants no one to love her, and to love no one. It's important that nothing make her hesitate.

When her family has left the house and she's the only person within its weatherboard walls—although presumably her father is somewhere, in the garage or the bathroom or reading the paper at the kitchen table—she sits cross-legged on the floor and closes her eyes. Outside and inside the house it's a dry, silent morning. She sits in cotton pyjamas, head bowed, her mousey hair pooling in the angles of her elbows. She thinks over the endless life she has lived, how it reached into the lives of her mother and father before she was born, how it reaches back to when Elizabeth and Joe were children and beyond this, too, to before *they* were born. She's lived just nearly thirteen years, but she has been in existence forever. Every twist of history brought her closer to being. And now, today, because of her, there is the weatherboard house; because of her, five children are on their unwilling way to church, bickering, laughing, plotting. *She* is responsible—Rex Jenson had scoffed and told her she was thinking wrong, and she's grateful that he tried, but maybe he is too kind to admit or perhaps even see such a bleak truth. She, however, can accept the facts. She was born, and in being so she chained up her parents; and they are miserable for it, and her siblings pay for the misery. This is *fact.*

If there is to be a new baby born into the family, so be it: the prospect only makes Freya more determined. With a baby, they can start fresh. The new one will never know what its brothers and sisters have known. When they tell stories, years from now, the youngest member of the family will struggle to believe.

She opens her eyes, a touch disappointed to find herself still in pyjamas on the floor. On the walls above her hang Marigold's drawings of foals, cats, big-eyed and wasp-waisted girls. Scattered about are her sisters' playthings, and Dorrie's pillow has flopped off the bed. There's a pattern in the carpet to which Freya has never paid any attention. Red roses on a grey background, and the carpet is scurfy in spots.

"I am sorry," she says. "I'm sorry, Mum. I'm sorry, Dad."

Everything will be different, after. She won't be able to retreat into the rooms of the castle which have kept her protected so far. It is daunting, and she is daunted, but she will not waver. Life is long, and this must end.

On Sunday afternoon the backyard of the Jensons' house returns to the birds. Sparrows light on the pool's white rim and hop forward for a drink. A blackbird flings worms from the churned soil at the base of the bike ramp. A magpie in its feathery tuxedo takes the deck steps one at a time.

Rex makes no comment on the quietness of the house. Colt watches him, trying to know what he knows. His father could easily decide that all the neighbourhood is busy elsewhere on this particular day. He could believe that the silence is nothing to do with him. And yet: he is not ignorant, he can't be ignorant. There can't be calmness inside him, it would not be fair. "Colt," he says, beckoning his son, and maybe there is a twinge in his voice like something dead receiving a tiny electric shock, "I'll give you five dollars if you can do this crossword puzzle."

Colt looks at the newspaper opened on the table: its puzzle is too difficult for him, he's tried before and earned only humiliation. "No thanks," he says.

Instead of teasing him, his father says, "Ten."

And there it is, nearly inaudible, the dead-man's jerk. Colt would like his father to be a dead man, or at least a man he's never met; he would like to strip from every atom in himself its inheritance of him. "No thanks," he says. And leaves his father sitting at the blondwood table.

Outside, the air is warm — this will be a hot summer. Colt walks through the heat with spread fingers and upturned palms. The Jensons sometimes take their holidays overseas, to beach resorts where the thatched huts have few walls and drinks are served in coconut shells and the meals are sliced straight from the flank of a rotisseried animal. Colt, with his olive skin, turns as brown as a local, his hair bleaches gold. His long legs kick aside the heft of an entire ocean. There has been no mention of a holiday this year. The new house has been enough change of scenery.

He goes to the shed, to where his bike stands; he thinks he'll go down to the creek. Not to the drain, but further along, following the tumbling water deep into the wasteland. There must be more to that wilderness than just the noxious pipe. There will be tracks among the weeds, caves in the banks, collapsed treetrunks bridging the water. It is time he explored. If he is to be alone, he needs to have places to be.

He's wheeling the red racer past the shed door when he pauses, looking back. Inside the shed it's dim, only a blade of light angling into it through the shunted-sideways door. Big shadows hulk across the ceiling and metal walls. Where the BMX usually stands — where it had been standing yesterday, when Colt was last here — the shadows are greyly empty, like the heart of a ghost. For an instant he thinks Bastian may have taken the bike out on his own, but that is nonsensical. There are some things Bastian does not do. Colt stares around the shed and back to where the dirtbike should be; then he props the racer on the path and walks around the garden. He looks under bushes, under the house, even into the pool. Birds dart from his path, the breeze swills warmly. When he returns to the shed, the bike is still missing.

Its absence opens a circular wound inside him which grows larger and more contaminating throughout the day. Panic rises and subsides in the wound, threatening to rush over the brim before sinking rapidly, only to rise lagoonishly again. He lurks in the playroom piecing together the train track, much to Bastian's delight. He makes the geography of the train's journey elaborate, with hills and tunnels built from books. On another day he might plant the odd suicidal soldier or rig up a landslide of tennis balls, but today his energy deserts him abruptly and he finds himself sitting with his back to the wall, hardly able to lift a hand. The limber black snake of a train runs past his toes and beneath the shelves as Bastian, on his stomach in the centre of the room, wrenches the switches tyrannically.

Over dinner he listens to the conversation of his parents — the dental surgery is having its gas supply cut off for a day while the pipes in the street are replaced. It's a massive inconvenience — "It's no laughing matter," says Rex, and laughs raucously: "Get it, Bas?" he asks, and the boy doesn't — but it has to be done. Colt would like to burst from his chair and hurl his plate at his father's head. "That's a massive inconvenience," he would scream, "but it had to be done!" Instead he eats patiently, one bean at a time, and when fear swells inside the wound he draws a breath and lets it out slowly, and the dread doesn't vanish but it comes under control.

But as night closes the world in, fear is difficult to evade. It rolls and eddies in his chest. It isn't bedtime but he lies beneath his sheets, his body flushing hot and cold. There's a high whine in his head which will only get louder, so he listens while he can to the sounds in the house. Bastian is singing a song that carries past the walls, something he's learned in music lessons at school. Bastian matters; he is odd and he is useless, more a burden than anything else. He is not a companion, he's just something to be cared for and worried about, like a hollow painted egg or a delicate captive fish. But there is no meanness in him, and he wants only that everyone should be happy—that's all he asks for, something as grand and humble as that. Something as idiotic and generous as that. Bastian matters, and Colt breathes until he can breathe again.

His mother passes the door, and stops at the sight of her son in his bed. "Are you ill, Colt?" she asks, and he tells her he's just tired. He could tell her about the theft of the BMX, but there is no point. She is not the person to do anything about anything. She is the person whose eyes are closed. He doesn't know the exact moment when he finally gave up on her—it must have come and gone like a ripple, leaving no change on his life. Tabby will stand by her husband even though he's someone against whom it's perilous to lean, who will drag her down with him when he falls. He has done it before, but still she clings to him. And Colt doesn't care if she does so out of fear of her husband or of the future or because she believes in loyalty above everything; he doesn't care if she's doing the best she can. He is never going to forgive her for the choice she has made. He says nothing, and soon she goes away.

Bastian comes to the door, gripping the doorframe with his fingers and hanging his weight off his arm. He is leggy, growing out of his pyjamas; ankles like fine ivory puzzles poke beyond the cuffs. His hair is long, how he likes it, his face the cleanest ever to shine on the world. "What are you doing, Colly?" he asks, and Colt answers, "Not much, just lying here."

Bastian thinks about this, and finds it inviting. He unhooks his fingers and comes into the room. Colt's bedroom is a holy citadel for the boy, a place of worship. He looks at the books and medals, precious articles he has no desire to touch. He would inherit them if Colt were to die, he'd keep them in boxes that he would cart with him for the length of his life, long after he'd forgotten the sound of Colt's voice and the colour of his eyes and even how it was, to have a brother. He drinks his fill of the marvellous things, then turns to Colt and graces him with a smile. "Good night," he says. "Sleep tight."

Because Dorrie and Marigold can't endure the wait one second longer, they put up the Christmas tree. It's a plastic tree which, dismantled, does not lie tidily in its box, and looks, in pieces, less like a tree than a knot of fossilised, murk-coloured lightning. But when they've fitted the trunk together and stood it on its stand, and squeezed the larger branches into the holes in the trunk and fitted, to the branches, the countless barbs of moulded greenery, the thing looks sufficiently like a tree to be worthy of the decorations that pour from their box as a tangled multitude. There are lengths of tinsel, gold, red and blue, and a string of fairy lights. There are matchboxes wrapped to look like gifts, and wooden animals of no discernible species. There are tinny, coloured-metal baubles, most of which have lost their strings. There are five very ancient decorations that Elizabeth bought before the children were born, peculiar people made from a substance like mirrored glass, with ugly painted faces and cuffs of shedding rabbit fur. These mirror people are both entrancing and repellent. The children don't like the way their mother smiles at them: yet they also wish there were many more, a vast community of the mirrored. They know there was once a sixth of their kind, the luckless one who met its fate in Freya's toddler fist in a tale which has become a legend.

The assembling and decorating of the tree should take less time than it does, but squabbling children draw out the job past dinner and into dusk. The tinsel must be hung so as to look casual, not roped about the tree like a measuring-tape around a fat lady. The decorations must be positioned so there is something of interest wherever the eye falls, although the best decorations must of course take pride of place at the front. The angel at the summit will not stand straight, and every Christmas the children complain about the abjectness of this creature. Elizabeth says, "Maybe we'll get some new things for next year," but next year never comes, and Syd is beginning to suspect his mother intends to keep the crippled seraph and assorted drab gewgaws forever. He's starting to see there is history in them: but he is ten, and there are more important things than the past. He finds himself daydreaming about what the Jensons' tree must look like: something opulent, probably real, high as the ceiling and strung with fat frosted tinsel and lights which flash different colours, and not an angel but a star with silver spikes like cavalry swords. And then he realises he's in danger of never seeing this splendid tree, just as he might never again visit the playroom, swoop over the bike jump, ride the red-and-white skateboard, or swim alone in the pool. There is a public pool not far away, and he likes it well enough: but the Jensons' pool had been his. Nobody knew it, but the pool belonged to him. Under the water, everything had stopped. Now, if the pool is gone, it will all go unrelentingly on.

The decorating of the Christmas tree had cheered him, but now grimness descends. He wanders out to the yard, to where Declan and Avery are kneeling on the path beside a bucket of water repairing a puncture in the front tyre of Declan's bike. Fixing a puncture is a job Joe does willingly, but Syd knows that his brother prefers to ask the least of their father that he can. The bike stands upside-down, balanced on its handlebars and saddle looking beached and vulnerable. The tube has been prised from inside the tyre to hang like a flaccid entrail, but when Declan screws the handpump to the valve and squirts air through it, the tube pops up like a Hula-Hoop. Now is the time to pass the tube through the water and it must be a more difficult task than it looks because Declan wrestles with this rubber anaconda, and water splashes the path and his trousers. "Want help?" Syd offers, because Avery is sitting on his scrawny haunches doing nothing, but Declan says, "No, it's OK."

It's Monday evening, and the brothers haven't spoken much since Saturday, when, with Garrick, they'd met Colt on the road, and left him standing there. The silence between them has caused Syd some pain, but it's important that Declan understand how angry and disappointed Syd is with him. Nevertheless, he has only one big brother. It is time to reopen the lines of communication. "We finished putting up the tree," he says.

"Hmm." Inch by inch Declan is feeding the tube through the water, having the hang of it now.

"So Dorrie can stop pestering Mum."

Declan frowns: a bubble has risen but it is difficult to tell if it came from the puncture or was merely a breath of trapped air. Avery murmurs his opinion, and Declan's search resumes. Syd scrapes the footpath, presses flat a leafy weed growing from a crack. From the house behind him comes a thump, a child's incensed squeal. "Nice night for a swim," Syd remarks.

"You're not going up there," his brother replies.

Syd stares at him—at both of them, Declan with his fringe over his eyes, Avery with his scabby knee. At school all the girls love Declan, he is so gallant, a sheriff from a midday movie; no one moves through life with more nonchalance than Avery. Syd has always been inexpressibly proud to have Declan for a brother and Avery for a friend: but on that Saturday morning, when they'd cruised away from Colt, he had been ashamed. "It was mean," he blurts out, "what we did!"

A flotilla of pinpoint bubbles shivers in the water, and Avery says, "Mmph." Declan clamps the hole and lifts the tube from the bucket. He drapes it across the concrete and, taking up a cloth, carefully dries the punctured place. Without looking at his brother he says, "Avery had to come with us. No one can be there alone."

"You could have stood up to Garrick." Syd feels fervid and aggrieved, he can't speak fast enough. "You could have said that we'd stay with Colt, and made *Garrick* go away."

Declan hunches to inspect the tube, the puncture that's a minute dot. He has their father's repair kit flipped open at his side, and he picks from it the metal file. Wrapping the tube around his knuckles, he scuffs the punctured area just enough to ruffle the rubber, and wipes the grit away. "I couldn't," he says. "Garrick is our friend—"

"No, I hate him!"

"—and what Mr. Jenson does is wrong."

Syd clamps his mouth shut. He watches his brother squeeze glue from a tiny bottle onto the scuffed place on the tube, then take the patching piece that Avery offers and press this into the glue. Syd wonders where he's recently seen something so painstaking and clinical, and remembers the man tending Avery's knee. "How long does the glue take to dry?" he asks, although he knows from experience it's no time at all.

"A few minutes." Declan looks at Avery, who agrees, "About."

Declan lays the tube on the footpath and sits back, surveying his work. With one hand he tips the bucket over, and water washes into the grass. It's still light, but if Syd were to look away for three or four minutes he would look back to find that night had arrived. "Colt is our friend too," he says, but lamely, the fight going out of him. "You like Colt, Deco. You like him more than you like Garrick."

"Yeah."

"So you should have remembered whose side you're on."

Declan probes the patch with a fingertip, and it shifts fractionally. He frowns, adjusts the patch back into place. "I'm on your side, Syd," he says. "Who else's side would I be on?"

And Syd doesn't say he's supposed to be on the side of the weak, because standing in the still yard with the upturned bike and the waning light it suddenly seems that everyone is weak, his sisters with their plastic tree, Syd with all his wishful dreams, Colt alone in the middle of the road, even Garrick Greene with his brutal brothers and surly mind and the money he needs to keep the friendship of his friends: they are, all of them, bumping along as helplessly as the silver balls in a pinball machine. And Avery, who's the most helpless and unmoored of them all, yawns and says, as if it's the most casual thing, "Garrick's stolen the BMX."

The Kiley boys look up. "What?"

"He stole it on Saturday night. It's under his house. I've seen it."

"Holy shit!" says Declan.

The news makes Syd clap his hands to his head. The insult — the very thought of it, Garrick's grubby paws groping that beautiful bike — makes him almost dizzy. "Why?" he asks, although as he asks he discovers he knows perfectly well why: "Because of what the man did?"

"I guess. And because of Colt."

"Because of Colt? It's not Colt's fault —"

"Nope." Avery shifts on the concrete; there's no fat protecting his bones. "But Garrick is in love with Colt. That's what's *really* making him mad."

The Kiley brothers goggle: Syd feels his brain tumble like a pup running after something it can't catch. Then Declan laughs. "What do you mean, he loves Colt?"

"Don't you reckon he does?" Avery smiles beatifically. "He always wants to be around Colt. He's always asking where Colt is, what he's doing, when he's coming home. He goes to Colt's house all the time, even though it's not the kind of place he'd usually be. He loves him."

Declan thinks about this, and says again, "Holy shit!"

"He doesn't *want* to love him. He hates Colt, because he loves him. And now he hates him even more, because if it wasn't for Colt then he wouldn't be anywhere near Colt's dad. So it is Colt's fault, see? So he has to make Colt sorry. He wants to be the boss of Colt, not for Colt to be the boss of him. He wants everything to be the way he's used to it being. So he stole the bike."

Declan goes to answer, but no words come out: he spreads his hands in wonder. Syd, too, gapes at Avery, who sits with his bare arms looping his knees, skinny and slightly grimy, innocent as grass and as shrewd as a leprechaun. All Syd can manage to ask is, "How do you know?"

Avery's ashy eyes glance at him and Syd catches sight of it fleetly, the scarred and slick side of a world he'll never live in. "It was just there," says Avery.

When she hears the car pull into the driveway she gets ready; part of her was hoping he would never come home. It's Wednesday, payday, early evening, not late for him. She listens as he moves into the house, his footsteps always random at first, as if he's never been here before, and his greetings to the girls which sound as if he's never met them: "Yes, hello Marigold, how are you, Dorrie." She hears her mother's voice and, below all of it, the yammer of the TV. She sits on the edge of her bed, her hands under her thighs. She hears him go to the kitchen and inspect the dinner put aside for him. She sees it all happening in her mind but feels a kind of blindness, and a sense that she's stopped existing as herself, Freya Kiley, and become instead a kind of sneaky insect whose squeezing in under the door brings destruction to the house. But it's not, she reminds herself, only good things that can end.

When he goes into the lounge room without bothering to eat the meal she stands up immediately and walks the length of the hall to the lounge, passing on her journey the bathroom, her brothers' room, her parents' room, the front door and the kitchen — the entire house. Her house, in every way. Bought because she had to be brought home. She's endured such guilt, and now she must do this terrible thing to make amends: but really, she hasn't only taken.

"Hello, Dad," she says.

He is standing with his back to her, propped against Syd's armchair and watching the television. Her mother is there, and all her siblings, the three youngest stretched out on the carpet. It takes a second for her voice to register, and when it does he turns awkwardly. "Hello, Freya."

"Drunk again," she says.

It's as if she's thrown a rattlesnake to the floor: there's a collective recoil and intake of breath. Marigold looks at her with wide-open eyes, Syd yanks his feet up under him. Freya presses on; she had known it wouldn't be easy. "I don't know why you come home when you're drunk. No one wants you here."

Marigold cries, "Oh, Freya!"

"Well, we don't. He stinks. He's revolting."

Joe says, "Watch your mouth, you little bitch."

She has never been sworn at by an adult, and it's disconcerting almost to the point of being derailing. But she tightens her fists and holds her ground and says, "What a pig you are."

To Syd it must appear that his sister has gone crazy: he's kneeling on the armchair saying, "Freya, no no—"

"Be quiet, Freya!" warns their mother. "Get out of here."

"Why?" Freya whirls to her. "Why do I have to be quiet? Why can't I tell him he's disgusting?"

But even as she speaks she is taking small steps in reverse because her father is advancing on her with equally small steps, and her heart has become a sparrow in a cage slamming at her ribs for escape. She sees how much bigger and stronger he is — much bigger than when they fix the station wagon together, much stronger than when he cooks her pikelets for breakfast. Not the same person: the knowledge both alarms and whips her on. He's closer, just three steps away, near enough that she can see the button undone on his shirt. "You make me sick!" she cries. "I'm embarrassed to have you as a father!"

"Get out," he sneers. "Get to bed—"

"No!" She shouts it as loudly as she can. "*You* get to bed! Get out of this house! I've had enough!"

His arm flies out, swinging as if to smash her from his sight but colliding with the Christmas tree, which collapses sideways without any resistance at all, hitting the carpet with a spiritless huff. Decorations spill from it, the angel capsizing from the peak. The entire family stares at it, the stubby upended cone of plastic suddenly seeming the worst of omens. Then Dorrie unleashes a godless wail, and Peter throws his head back and howls too, and Freya screeches at her father, "Now look what you've done!"

Joe glares, his head tossing as though he'd shake off what he hears like bees. Then, "Get out!" he yells. "Out of my sight!"

"Freya, stop!" says their mother, and there's no fear or pleading in her voice, just an iron intolerance Freya hasn't heard before. Declan has jumped up from the couch, Dorrie and Marigold and Peter are shrieking a noise like a whirlwind. Joe swings a splayed hand, and Freya darts out of reach—but she's misjudged something, her house has turned against her, the yellow-eyed monster that hunts her suddenly snags her in its claws, because instead of slipping lithely past the door she hits the doorframe and for the tiniest instant she is trapped, unable to take the step that would carry her beyond reach. And this man whom she has never seen looms in front of her before she can raise her hands, a man who so clearly despises her that it sucks the air from her lungs and the strength from her legs. His fist is up, a solid mallet aimed at her drained face. "Oh no," she gabbles, "no, don't—" and then the room itself seems to roar. *"Do not!"* says their mother. *"Don't you dare!"* And Elizabeth is there, gripping her husband's arm and pulling him back with irresistible force. "Don't you dare hit her!" So Freya's father hits her mother instead, an unhesitating punch to the jaw which makes a deadly sound and slings their mother like a soft doll into the wall. And the cries of the children become colliding screams of terror, Freya glimpses them scuttling on their knees as her mother buckles to the floor. Declan dives beside her, but Freya does not wait to see more: she turns and bolts from the room, out the front door and across the garden and into the open street. She's young and fit, she can run like an animal and that is how she's imagined it, flying up the hill the way a deer would sprint the distance in an effortless gallop: in fact she runs in agony, tears streaming down her face, sobbing into herself great painful gallons of air. The evening is hazy, the streetlights are on, but it isn't yet dark and some birds are out, swooping and weaving ahead of her as she stumbles along the path. She struggles to go faster but it's the running of a nightmare, her legs are as heavy as anvils, each stride requires all her strength yet seems to propel her nowhere. She's turned the corner and is labouring uphill and she can see the front fence of the Jensons' house, their porch light beyond the trees, but it's almost impossible to haul herself closer and she understands the monster has curved its paw around her heel and is toying her inevitably into its embrace. Something has gone disastrously wrong, her poor mother thrown to the wolf, and Freya is nothing but a stupid child who pulled the bolt that held back something infinitely more ferocious than she.

And then she is charging up the concrete steps and hammering on the Jensons' door. In her mind she's always seen Rex but in real life it is Tabby who opens the door. Her pretty face drops at the sight of the girl: "Freya! What's happened?"

"My dad is killing my mum!" she bawls.

And suddenly Rex is also there, appearing behind his wife with a frown across his handsome brow. "Calm down, Freya, just be calm—"

"No!" she yells. "You have to help us! It's my fault, I didn't mean it, he's hurting her—please, please!"

In her dreams he'd dashed out in a flurry of something like eagle feathers; instead he looks her up and down and she sees him hesitate. His mouth opens and closes over white teeth, and Tabby says, "Call the police, Freya. That's what you must do."

Rex nods rapidly. "Yes, that's the thing. Call the police. It's not my place to interfere."

She rocks on her feet. "But Mr. Jenson—I need you—"

He says, "What specifically do you expect of me?"

"Call the police," says Tabby. "Don't get involved, Rex."

Freya looks from her, this miserable woman, to him, who should be rising on wings but instead is lurking—almost hiding—behind his wife. They stare back at her from the dark side of the door, their admirable faces empty. Expecting her gone, now they've told her what to do. Repulsed that she's brought this to their doorstep, but ready to forgive if she will go away. Otherwise, it is over. She blinks into this new blond light, says, "There's no time to call the police."

"I'll come with you, Freya." It is Colt: he slips between his parents and out the open door. "No!" says Tabby, and grapples for him, but already he's beyond her reach; and although Rex says, "Colt, listen!" he doesn't pause, but takes the steps two at a time, and his father does not try to catch him. And Freya, her hands knotted at her mouth, gives Rex a last glance, because it is him she needs—a grown man—even if he's not the man she came looking for, which is something she will never forget. And Rex looks pained and says, "Oh, for goodness sake," and follows his son out the door, and Tabby throws her hands up and spins away as if she's witnessed something beyond describing.

But Freya's heart leaps—sluggishly, but it leaps. It leaps and lurches down the street with Colt and Rex, and part of her finds it blackly amusing that her plan is going so haywire while also managing to stay largely on track. Rex is coming to the rescue, but everything has been lost. She's unbolted a castle door and found not only a monster, but that she's a monster herself.

At the white house the screen door is open, and Dorrie is standing on the veranda in her pink nightdress and bare feet: she bleats when she sees Freya, her arms reaching up, but Freya storms past without stopping. Her father is in the kitchen stomping about randomly, and he has made his usual mess—cutlery is scattered, food has been buffeted from its plate, chairs have fallen over, one cupboard door has been kicked off a hinge. The kitchen smells like he does, of cigarette butts and dregs. Elizabeth is on a chair in the lounge room, a wet cloth pressed to her jaw, and Syd and Marigold and Peter are clustered round her, Peter clinging to his brother, Marigold with her head on her mother's lap. Declan is hovering nearby, gripping the neck of a heavy vase that was a wedding present to Elizabeth and Joe. His face is pale and he looks at Freya as if she's unknown to him. The television is still loyally screening, indifferent to being ignored. Freya halts in the hallway junction where the lounge and kitchen meet, and Rex steps up behind her. In his arms he's carrying Dorrie, whose small hands push against his chest. He looks over Freya's head to Joe, and Freya knows, although she can't see and has never seen it, that he has no idea what to do. "Ah," he says. "Joe. Hello."

Freya's father has barged into the wall near the stove; at the sight of Rex he plants a foot against the plaster and levers himself away. His hair is mussed but otherwise he looks like her father again. "Good evening, Mr. Dentist," he says. "What brings you here? Bleeding gums? Rotten molar? Would you care for some dinner? A drink?"

Dorrie squirms to be put down but Rex keeps her to him.

"No thanks, Joe, I've eaten. And I don't drink on a work night. Nothing worse than a dentist with shaky hands."

But Joe is not listening. He looks around at the smeared food, the listing cupboard, the newspapers on the floor. "It's a mess in here," he says. "Is your house a mess, Rex?"

"Sometimes, Joe."

"You'd think it wouldn't be hard to keep a house tidy. I don't know what she does all day."

"That I can't tell you," says Rex.

Dorrie kicks frantically, and Rex puts her down. The girl bolts to her mother, shoving Marigold aside. Elizabeth, Freya sees, has closed her eyes, as if the scene is wearying. Colt stands further down the hall in the shadows, as silent as if he's not there. Joe says, "I've been thinking about that deck around your swimming pool. You want to get it built as soon as you can. I can get you some second-hand timber, or do you want new?"

"Either is fine," says Rex. "Anything that will do the job."

Freya's father nods; he looks down at his dinner plate. The chops and potato have sloshed over the rim and only a scatter of peas remains, trapped in a streak of tomato sauce. "Can I get you a drink, Mr. Dentist?" he asks.

"Dad!" Freya shouts. "You hit Mum!"

Joe lifts his head and blinks incuriously at her. He takes a long moment to respond. "Rex," he says, "I don't know if you've met my eldest daughter, Freya. She speaks whether spoken to or not. You mightn't want to meet her, actually."

Freya does not flinch. "You hit Mum," she says stonily.

"Don't be stupid—"

"Dad!" cries Declan, and Elizabeth opens her eyes.

"Well, Joe," Rex says, "I think you did. I'm sure you didn't want to, and maybe you don't remember, but it seems you did."

Joe's blue gaze moves over him—over his face and chest and arms. Rex is tall, with long athletic limbs, and Joe is a small man: but Rex is like a tree branch, and Joe is made of stone. "Who said so?" he asks.

"Well, Freya said. I can see the evidence."

"Freya said," Joe echoes, "and you can see the evidence. What evidence? Evidence of what? You were here, were you, or do you just believe what you're told? Who are you anyway?" he says, and although he hasn't moved a step away from the table, each word is bringing him closer. "Who are you to come in here, into my own kitchen, and accuse me of doing something without proof?"

"Dad!" says Freya. "Stop lying! Look at Mum!"

"Tell the truth!" says Elizabeth.

"You're right, you're right." Rex's hands have come up. "Let's not have any trouble. This is your house, Joe, and I agree it's not my place to tell you what to do. But the children are upset. Maybe it's best to say good night. Go and sleep it off, hey?"

From across the kitchen Joe regards him and Freya knows the look, the dull loveless light that is what's left when her father has gone. "I should throw you out on your arse," he says, and gives the plate a shove which sends it rushing to the edge of the table. "Throw you and every one of them out into the street."

"It's probably better if you went—"

"Is it? Is it, mate? How are you gonna make me? Fight me?"

Rex gives a short tight laugh, and then he takes it, just a tiny step backwards, his shoes never leaving the carpet: but Freya feels a canyon open around her. "I'd rather not. I'm a friend, Joe. I don't mean you any harm, there's no need to be unpleasant. But I would advise you to either leave the house or go to bed. It's best for everyone, yourself included. I'm going to stay here until you do one or the other."

Joe appears to muse on this, his eyes rolling to the ceiling. Dorrie has stopped whimpering and the only sound comes from the yacking television. Then: "Rex." Joe wags a finger at their neighbour. "I remember you."

"I hope so." Rex smiles. "I need you to help me build the deck."

Joe grins in return, and it is unnerving. He grins and says, "Yeah, I remember," and points his finger like a pistol. "You've been touching my kids."

Freya feels it like a punch to the face. "Dad!"

"I beg your pardon?" says Rex.

Joe jabs his finger, standing straighter now, smiling his wire smile. "Yes, you have. Been touching my kids. You come into my house, tell me what I should do, telling lies, threatening me, acting like some kind of *hero* . . . and you've been touching my kids!"

The men stare at each other across the kitchen, and the air between them could burn. Elizabeth makes a muffled noise and turns away, but Freya's brothers and sisters are as mute and still and wan-faced as children in an ancient painting. Rex, too, is very still: then, "Aha," he says, and gives a slight bob of his head. He squares his shoulders and says stoutly, "I think you've been misinformed, Joe."

Freya's father answers instantly. "No, I don't think so. My boys say you can't keep your mitts to yourself."

Rex goes to speak, but is silent; then says, "I'm not exactly sure what you're implying, but whatever it is, it's simply untrue—"

"Calling my kids liars, are you? A bloke like you?"

"Now, Joe," says Rex, "let's not get insulting. Let's not get out of hand—"

"Declan!" Joe shouts. "Sydney! Come here!"

"Dad," mutters Freya, "please don't—"

Joe, if he heard, disregards her, banging his palm on the table. "Declan! Sydney!"

The boys, in the lounge room, look at their mother, who shakes her head and murmurs, "Ignore him." And Syd does, edging nearer her, wrapping his arms tighter around Peter. But Joe hammers the table, calling, "Declan! Deco! Declan, come here!" and Declan comes warily forward, stopping in the doorway beside Freya. His hand is still clutching the throat of the vase; he is as white as a boy in a tower. "What, Dad?" he says.

"Deco. Declan." Joe grins at him, and his pistol of fingers comes up again. "Mr. Dentist, this is my son, Declan. Declan, take a look at that man there. He's calling you a liar."

Rex, for the first time, looks at Declan: and reaches out a hand to grasp Declan's shoulder, and seems to stand taller for doing so. To Joe he says deeply and calmly, "I know Declan, Joe, and I would never call him a liar. I think extremely highly of him, and

I'm also very fond of him. I know he's a good boy, a credit to you and your wife. So, with respect, I'd like to hear what Declan has to say from his own mouth, not from yours, Joe. Declan," he says, and pulls Declan slightly sideways so he can look down into the boy's face, "your father has just made a very unpleasant claim in your name. Now I would like to ask you: have I ever, in any way, behaved in a manner that's caused you concern? Have I—as your father puts it—*touched* you?"

Rex looks down with his honest, amber eyes, but Declan only glances up at him before his gaze slides away, passing Freya to find Colt in the shadows. Colt, discovered, does not flinch or run. Declan stares at him; then his sights lurch back to Joe. He looks at his father, and later Freya will wonder if, in these seconds, he's remembering the times Joe has commanded him to get to bed because the very thought of the unspoiled life ahead of his son is hateful and enviable and riling to Joe: or if it's some other reason completely that makes him answer as he does. "What was that, Deco?" Rex says, giving the boy's shoulder a gentle shake. "Could you speak louder, please, so your father can hear?"

Declan's face, which was bloodless, is now blazing, but he speaks again obediently, louder and more clearly. "No," he says, "that's not true." Then he slips from Rex's grasp, out of the cramped junction of the doorway, and Rex lets him go. To Joe he spreads his hands imploringly, as tall as the ceiling now: the television sounds abruptly maddening, the house crowded to the hilt, and their father, beside the table, has blurred around the edges. He blinks at Rex, grasping and ungrasping the back of a chair. "Well done," he says. "Nicely done."

Rex, all confidence, says, "This situation is of your making, Joe."

"Is it. Is it. Is that what it is." Joe smiles. "What was it," he says, "that I am supposed to do? I've forgotten."

"Just go to bed, friend. Sleep it off."

Joe nods and smiles, squeezing the chair. "Big hero," he says.

"Someone has to be," answers Rex.

Joe shoves the chair away. "Fucking superman," he sighs. Maybe, Freya will think, he could have fought harder, but he pushes off from the table and walks out the back door without another word. And the sorrow her heart eternally carries for him flames devastatingly, so she almost cries out: she rushes to the window to watch him cross the yard and thinks, *Oh my dad, I'm sorry.* She watches until she hears his car drive away, and when she turns she sees that Rex has crouched beside Elizabeth and is inspecting her damaged face: Elizabeth is mumbling, "Thank you, Rex," and he's replying, "Oh, happy to help, glad I could be of help." And Freya sees it as if fluorescently lit, how he has them in his clutches now, that whatever he wants they must give him. She sees their future—the walks to church, the saintly smiles, the beige wall, the blank screen, the silvery instruments in his hands—and feels herself rusting inside. The yellow-eyed monster with its slinky black limbs has chased her right into her home. *I'm sorry,* she pleads to whoever might hear. *Help me, please, I'm sorry.*

Colt stays inside when he comes home from school, playing cards or doing more homework than he's been assigned. Outside is no longer part of his domain. Outside, on the street, he might cross the path of the neighbourhood boys, and that would be more than he can tolerate; moreover, outside risks putting the thought of the BMX into his father's head. He can't keep the bike's disappearance secret forever. His father is not the sort of person who forgets—he's always going to take an interest in the bike. So Colt stays inside, killing time, wondering if this is what his life will be: a bedroom, a bookshelf, a window.

And sometimes the unfairness of it makes him wonder why he's keeping the disappearance a secret at all: it's not Colt who made the bike go missing. He should tell his father, and then tell him why. But since the moment Declan said that word *no,* Colt has watched his father swell as if he's unhinged his jaw and swallowed a massive, fleshy meal that he's been hungering to eat. His father will say Colt is mistaken. He'll say Colt's lack of faith is more hurtful than that of anybody else. Then he will demand the names of those who knew where the bike was kept, and he'll feel the need to summon each of these to a suburban inquisition in the kitchen, charging no one with the crime but explaining how the theft has spoiled the memories they share. And if he does this, Colt must die. His will to live will drain away, and he will die.

And something else could happen, something which is possible because it's happened before. His father won't recognise when enough is enough, he'll joke and chuckle and pleasantly, politely, inescapably insist until somebody stops laughing, and then the loss of the bike will be nothing compared to what comes next. The knock on the door, the sheltered conversations: and the Jensons will leave, and at the next house there will be a cascade of toys to smooth over the dislocation and the distress, and to help them make new friends.

So he's cloistering himself to keep the bike's vanishment a secret, and to stop someone's patience wearing thin.

In the three days since he went with his father to the Kileys' his thoughts have returned obsessively to the white weatherboard and the children gathered around their mother in the lounge room. He had never been to the Kiley house before, and he keeps finding details that have snagged in his memory. The photographs hung in the hallway, their frames mismatched and inexpensive. The aluminium biscuit tin on the kitchen counter with its wonky green bakelite knob. The field of crumbs beneath the toaster, the cord frayed where it met the socket. Grey carpet, sparse in the passage where they must walk, patterned with ivy and blotched roses. The butter-yellow vinyl of the dining-table chairs, to one of which a child has taken a biro and drawn a crackle of blue. Standing in the hallway he'd concentrated on this scribble for minutes at a time, because it had been unbearable to look at Elizabeth and the children. He can't imagine looking at Declan ever again. It would be a kind of insult, and Colt has no wish to insult him more.

He had left the house unnoticed that night, and walked home alone through the tepid evening. His mother had been waiting anxiously by the window, and Bastian had been weeping without knowing why. To distract his brother, Colt had told him about the scribble on the yellow chair. Bastian had been shocked. "Bad children!" he'd said.

His mother had kept asking, "Is it all right? Colt? Is it all right? Colt?"

And when his father had come home not too much later he had been full of bravado, stuffed to the gills with the fleshy meal of satisfaction. Tabby had sat on the edge of the couch while Rex strode around the lounge room. "It was nothing!" he'd told her, almost shouting. "Really, it was a huge fuss about very little. He's comparatively harmless. The problem is that people don't appreciate how bad things can truly be."

Tabby said, so angrily, "That girl needs to learn that the world doesn't revolve around her."

"Oh, come now, she's only young. Still, I've no doubt they provoke him . . ."

"So it's their problem then. Next time they must sort it out themselves. Don't go looking for trouble, Rex."

"Well," said Rex, "we'll see." And Colt had wished that Joe

had raised a workingman's fist and slammed it into his father's face with the force of a freight train.

Now, on Saturday afternoon, he's sitting at his desk working on a list of places he'd like to go when he hears the familiar ting of a bicycle bell as tyres bump down the gutter. He sets aside his pen and hesitates, but he understands he is being invited, and he wants to go. First, however, he detours to the playroom and scoops up the red-and-white skateboard.

Syd is riding round randomly, as if there's a mouse on the road he wants to squash. Colt comes down the driveway, and Syd looks up. "Oh," he says. "Hi."

Colt can't believe how delighted he is to see the boy, but all he says is, "Hi."

Syd glides a circle, his eyes on the road. His glance goes to the skateboard, flicks away. "What have you been doing?"

Colt can't say he's been waiting, so he says, "Nothing."

"Me neither." Syd stops his bike before he sails past Colt again, plants his feet on the road. He looks up at the red-brick house, down to the flaking chrome of his handlebars. "How have you been?" Colt asks.

Syd shrugs. "OK."

"What about Declan?"

"Yeah, he's OK."

"Can you tell him . . ." Colt pauses; it is difficult. "Can you tell him I said sorry?"

Syd crinkles his nose. "You don't have to be sorry. It's just life, isn't it? That's what Deco says. You've just got to live with it."

Colt says, “I guess.” And because he’s sometimes found himself thinking about her he asks, “How’s Freya?”

“Hmm, the same.”

But Colt doubts this. “Will you tell her I said hi?” he says, and when the boy nods easily, adds, “Don’t forget.”

“I won’t. But you can tell her yourself the next time you see her.”

Colt smiles, looking away. The breeze rubs his face, the sun strokes his arms. He would tell the boy how he’s craved to see him and all that he means, and Syd might say the same. Instead they contemplate the road as if it will speak for them, and what Syd says is, “The BMX. Garrick’s got it.”

“Oh,” says Colt. “OK.”

Syd eyes him. “Aren’t you mad?”

Colt doesn’t know how he feels—he doesn’t think he’s mad. He thinks he’s always known Garrick Greene had the bike, and why. “Thanks for telling me.”

“I can try to get it back for you.”

“No, I’ll get it back.” And then, recalling the skateboard in his hands, he holds it out to Syd. “Here. You can have this.”

Instead of seizing it and haring off, the boy baulks. “Why?”

“Well . . . It could be a reward for telling me about the bike.”

Syd scowls. “I don’t need a reward. I hate Garrick. I don’t care if it’s dobbing. It serves him right.” But his eyes linger on the board, its stripes of blood and bone, and he licks his lip. “Maybe, after Christmas, if you still don’t want it, I’ll take it.”

Colt shoulders the board. “OK.”

Syd draws a steadying breath and smiles. "How's Bastian?"

"Oh, you know. Bastian."

"Tell him he better keep practising those slot cars if he wants to beat me."

There's a silence, the song of a bird. The boys look along the length of the street, at the closed-tight doors and windows, the cars that never leave. Syd twiddles idly with his bike's bell, casts a sidelong glance at the skateboard. "Anyway, I better go," he says. "I'll see you round, Colt."

"Yeah, see you," Colt says, and the boy pedals away. And Colt, who has grown so tired in these past cluttered weeks of bikes and pools and barbeques and drains and skateboards and ice-cream and sheds and wounded knees during which he's only ever been falling, falling, feels an anchoring sense of relief to finally be given a price he can pay.

So when, the following day, he watches Garrick ride up the driveway, he goes to the door and opens it before the boy can knock. He feels no fear, only a gratitude that Garrick should have chosen a public path. It's Sunday, and the afternoon is drowsy. "Hi," he says, and Garrick replies, "Are you looking for your bike?"

They ride side-by-side through the streets, keeping to the middle of the road. They pass people in their gardens and a small boy pedalling a tricycle along the footpath who shouts at them furiously, "Hiawatha!" A brown dog, investigating a naturestrip, lifts its ears as they pass. An old man is trimming a hedge with shears, a portable radio at his feet. A cricket match is being played somewhere, and the pleasing *thock* of the ball against the willow carries across the hills of the suburb. Colt's racer travels well, soundless but for the steady burr of its wheels on the bitumen. He is amazed by how reconciled he feels toward what is coming. He isn't afraid. He is willing.

Garrick says something, and Colt looks at him. The boy's cheeks are burnished by the wind, his fringe blown back from his forehead like black grass on a sandy dune. Garrick's bike does not have gears, and he has to stand on the pedals to force it up the hills. Out of courtesy, Colt does the same. He wants it this way: polite. When this day is over, he'll never speak of it again. "I didn't hear you," he tells Garrick, swooping the red racer closer, and Garrick says, "I heard your dad was a tough guy at the Kileys' the other night."

His tone is snide. "Did Declan say that?" Colt asks.

"Avery."

"That's not what happened," Colt tells him.

They pass house after house, wide gateless front gardens, cars parked on the street. A striped cat gallops across the road in front of them and Garrick curses it on its way. Colt knows where they are going, he could take the lead, but that isn't how it should be and he's careful not to hurry. For now, what they're doing is something like a game. "So how did you find the bike?" he asks Garrick, because the boy is playing too.

"Dunno. Just found it."

"Just lying there?"

"Yep." He throws a testy glance, and Colt settles into silence.

The wasteland along the creek is very green—outrageously green, to Colt's eye, the green from a child's finger-painting. Expanses of weed rise waist-high on either side of the path, forming dense fields of blinding emerald. It's almost impossible to walk through these fields; they see dents where exuberant dogs have romped, but otherwise the tangled swathes are thick and unbroken. Anything could be buried in the depths, woven into the roots, feeding the grass and becoming part of it. Midges hover above the tips of the weeds, striking Colt's face like fairies. Garrick pedals fast along the dusty track, but not so fast that Colt could not outride him. As soon as they put the bikes down, he could outrun him. But he doesn't stop or turn the racer around even though what's coming is suddenly much closer now they're here, and he feels an apprehension at the edge of his mind: he keeps riding, concentrating on the stones which burst away from Garrick's tyre and shoot off into the grass.

The weeds, as the breeze moves over them, make a rushing, heralding noise. The wind in the scrappy heads of the trees also whispers secrets. He cannot hear the water, the creek being almost soundless from even the smallest distance. A stranger to this place might never know it was flowing there.

He expects they are going to the drain, which is Garrick's lair, but they ride past the dark mouth of the pipe without stopping, and Colt corrects himself: of course it won't be here, because this is Garrick's lair. Garrick isn't silly. He is lazy, however, and unadventurous and unimaginative, so when they find the BMX it's not far from the pipe after all—looking back, Colt can see the top lip of the concrete mouth. He kicks down the stand of the racer and steps forward to investigate.

The BMX lies on its side in the weeds, two or three steps off the path. Its left handgrip and serrated pedal are its highest peaks. Weeds pike between its spokes and splay around the saddle. At a glance it seems undamaged: dry and clean, it hasn't lain in this place for long. Colt puts his hands on his hips, considering it. He remembers the evening his father brought the bike home, the hateful guessing-game they'd played. Not much more than a month has passed since then, but it has seemed to take longer, this final downhill run. "What colour do you reckon this bike is?" he asks Garrick.

The boy is standing on the path behind him, having thrown his own bicycle into the dust. Colt can smell him, a not unpleasant stink. Flammable, like petrol. "I dunno. Black?"

Colt smiles. A swarm of midges sweeps past, waltzing on the breeze, and he waves them away from his face. "I hate this bike," he tells Garrick.

"What? Are you crazy? That's a quality bike. There's nothing wrong with that bike."

"Maybe." Colt treads out of the grass to stand before Garrick. The sun is not deep into its afternoon descent, and the boys' shadows bunch to their feet. There is no one around, as far as Colt can see. No dogs poking about, no people to protest. He has perplexed and bothered Garrick by insulting the BMX, even hurt his feelings. "I'd let you keep it," he explains, "but I need it back."

Garrick lifts his gaze and studies him, his eyes moving lightlessly. He chews on something, his thoughts or memories, and his sights move, return, shift away. He frowns and cracks a knuckle. "I know it's not your fault," he says. "But he can't just . . . get away with it, and nothing ever happens."

"No, I know." Colt catches the boy's eye. "It's all right, Garrick. You should do it."

Garrick's lip jerks, he makes a resentful sound. "I don't want to," he says. "I like you, Colt. But you *knew.* You knew, and you didn't tell us. You let him."

Colt says, "I'm sorry—"

Garrick's face instantly curdles. "Piss off being sorry. Sorry is full of shit. You know what's the worst part? We could have been friends. I like you, you're a good guy. But now look what has to happen. What else can I do?"

"I don't know," says Colt, and truly he doesn't. Maybe this is the first of a life's worth of strange deals he will make, atoning any way he can because his mother and father will not, and Bastian should not have to. If this is how it must be, it is much better than nothing. He's ready to do what he can. "It's OK," he says. "Do it. You should. I want you to."

Garrick regards him suspiciously, unaccustomed to compliant victims. "I will," he says. "When I'm ready. Don't tell me what to do." He shuffles back and rolls his shoulders, wipes his nose on a wrist. He hefts his hands, bloats his cheeks and blows out air. He peers into the distance, looks behind to see if anyone is there; he scuffs toeholds into the path, scoops his fringe behind an ear. They might be here, Colt thinks, all day. He could provoke him by running, but the danger is he will accidentally escape. So he stays where he is, his shadow a dry pool at his feet, his face turned, politely waiting: yet when Garrick hits him the blow is shocking, a force which throws him almost off his feet. Garrick says nothing and makes no sound—either he's been taught to fight or has a natural talent or simply enjoys it, for he steps forward and delivers a second efficient punch which catches Colt under the ribs and drops him to his knees, palms skidding on the path and swilling up a witch of white dust. He glimpses Garrick's face—set now, doubt erased—as the boy swings a foot intent on bringing his adversary completely down. Colt's chin and elbow smack the path and a crisp sheet of pain cracks through his body, as well as a stringy, unstringing sense of panic. It is possible to die.

And then Garrick is on him, having resolved that the mighty fall with reason and that the weak invite their punishment and that anything, once begun, should continue wholeheartedly to the end: he drops onto Colt's chest, slamming the air from his lungs, arches back an arm and punches the boy as hard as he can. His fist rams first into Colt's cheekbone and, drawn back again like a piston, into his right eye; before Colt's hands can come up to protect him Garrick has landed another blow, this time to Colt's fine nose, the bone of which Colt feels splinter: blood splashes his face and Garrick's knuckles as if a pipe has burst. Blood does not frighten Garrick Greene: it strengthens him. He is snarling and heaving, swearing with each breath, remembering why he is here now, and burning with a kind of glory. He grips the collar of Colt's t-shirt and hoists the boy out of the dust, and with his blood-smeared fist drives a hideous blow into Colt's jaw. Blood bursts free from Colt's mouth and hits the path, and Colt hits the path also, no longer even trying to save himself.

It is difficult to decide when enough is enough. There is always a feeling that the next moment might be the great one, the one relived for a lifetime. Garrick's swearing blurs into frustrated babble. He doesn't know if he is done. He shakes Colt, knees him, afraid to make a mistake. He jabs Colt in the ribs and stomach, cuffs him around the ears, and finally flops on Colt's chest, shaking his fighting hand, which is throbbing, while he waits for his head to decide. Beneath his bullish weight, Colt struggles to breathe.

His mouth and throat are soupy with blood. Blood bubbles from his nose and oozes out his mouth. It has run down his throat into his t-shirt, and through the tangles of his torn hair. It is a brazenly red, protesting colour. Garrick shakes his head, squeezing his hand. He looks at the boy pinned between his knees: "Hey!" he says. "Hey! Is that enough?" The answer is evidently important because he asks again more loudly, staring into Colt's wincing eyes. "Hey! Is it enough? Is it?" And his victim's hoarse breathing must mean it is not enough, because Garrick makes a sound — a predator's noise, something between a growl and a hiss — and slams his fist against Colt's skull, into the place where the vulnerable points are. It seems blissfully easy to do it, he's unhampered by hesitation or care: but when it is done there's a sense of finality that drapes like a heavy curtain over their heads. He is spent and bleak now, it is as good as finished.

He slumps a while on Colt's ribcage, panting, head hanging. Then he clambers to his feet and stares down at his victim, clutching his hurting hand. Dust has smudged his hair, jeans and runners; attached on his chin is a pasty gob of spit. He swipes his mouth, shakes his hand. He tells Colt, "You asked for that."

Colt blinks and coughs and grimaces, sprinkling the air with blood. When he's gathered sufficient strength he twists onto his side, turning his back on his assailant. His body is being compressed by a peculiar pain, as if a cannon is rolling across it. His face feels made of glass ground underneath a heel. He does not want to hear Garrick's voice, even less the voice inside his own head. At this moment there is nothing that can make any of this all right. The path is coarse against his cheek, uncomfortable enough to assure him he is still alive. Beyond the odour of his own blood he smells crushed stone and chalk. But his breathing is ragged, as if he's dragging a cart uphill, and the air that is pulled past his leaking lips tastes of spit and blood. His teeth are wrapped in a pulp of gore, his spine is a burning wick. His hands have been stomped, the skin slewed from the bones, and he hugs them to his shallowly lifting chest. Already his pounded eye is puffing closed. He knows he is vulnerable lying here, and he feels Garrick looming, tempted, but there is nothing he can do. He is smashed in a hundred places, hardly brave enough to breathe. Maybe his mind drifts in these moments, because he sees himself as the universe, or sees a universe that is inside him: a trillion microscopic pieces spinning in a colourless space, each piece glowing like an orb of honey, a galaxy of golden fireflies. He feels the presence of Garrick Greene behind him and he nurses his aching body waiting for the world to decide if anything has been righted, but part of him glides painlessly through a gold-flecked universe, having left the dust behind.

Eventually he hears Garrick say, "I'll tell Declan you're here." The weeds make a ripping sound as the bike is pulled from among them. Air puffs from the padded seat, cogs squeak as they turn. The ground itself rumbles as the boy rides away.

When he thinks he can bear it, Colt opens his unharmed eye. The afternoon is aggressively bright and he closes his eye, draws a breath, cautiously looks again. He is lying by the path's edge, and the weeds are very near. This close, he sees all kinds of details, the fuzz that coats each green spike, the precise cleave down the centre of each blade, the network of roots grappling the earth, the intricate bed of rot. Tiny stones rise hugely, waxy pink, blue and green. There are scarlet plates on the path that he recognises as blood. The sun feels hot—scalding—against his face, yet his body is cold, and he drags his knees to his chest, tucks his skinned palms between his thighs. He lets his teeth chatter but only for an instant, because their collision is pain.

He is covered in grit and blood; tears stream from his eyes, and he doesn't know why. He's badly hurt, but pain has never made him cry. He's crying, he supposes, for another reason; but he will stop. By the time Declan finds him he will be sitting up, smiling woozily, able to talk without spraying ruby beads. The thought alone makes him feel somewhat repaired.

A microscopic insect, lesser than a flea, is moving down a string of weed. When it reaches a break in the stem it hesitates, spins a circle, trundles back the way it has come. Colt breathes in as deeply as he's able, then lets his chest carefully fall. He feels the spangling universe inside him, the embrace of the warm air around him, the reliable stone underneath. Tomorrow, if the weather is fine, he will run, swim, ride.